Praise for Ignite's Authors

Lori Verni-Fogarsi
"[*Momnesia*] is about being a good mom without losing yourself in the process. The author tackles the subject with humor and gets you thinking about a worthwhile subject...yourself!" ~*The Boston Globe (Boston.com Moms)*

Kelly Lawrence
On *Unconditional*: "Sweet, yet sizzling hot!" ~*Kirsty Mosely, bestselling author*

Katherine Crighton
"[*Salt and Silver*] is one of a kind. The action and romance [are] interlaced with humor, bringing a readability to tough topics." ~*Romantic Times Book Reviews, Top Pick, 4.5 Stars*

Michael Bracken
"Bracken's mystery fiction is of the tougher-minded sort." ~*Publisher's Weekly*

Brickstone Publishing
133 Clay Ridge Way, Suite #200
Holly Springs, NC, 27540
www.BrickstonePublishing.com

Library of Congress Control Number: 2013955944
Publisher Cataloging Data:
Verni-Fogarsi, Lori
      Ignite / Lori Verni-Fogarsi.—1st ed.
      p. cm.
      ISBN: 978-0-9840284-2-9

      1. Erotica—Fiction. 2. Romance—Fiction. 3. Anthology—Fiction. 4. Mothers—Fiction. I. Title.

BISAC: FIC027010
BISAC: FIC005000
BISAC: FIC003000

Designed & compiled by: Lori Verni-Fogarsi
Edited by: Clarice Joos

Building a solid foundation
for books and their authors.

Ignite

Compiled by

Lori Verni-Fogarsi

"Ignite" Authors

Michael Bracken

Alice Bright

Shenoa Carroll-Bradd

Katherine Crighton

Julianna Darling

Kelly Lawrence

Jen Lee

J.R. Read

Lizzie Richards

Lori Verni-Fogarsi

Table of Contents

Dedication

To all the moms of the world...

You work your butt off. You give of your time, your efforts, and most of all, your love. You make sacrifices, often forgoing your own interests in favor of your children's.

It is entirely possible that you're mistaken for a scullery maid and a short order cook, all while managing to act like you don't mind things such as wiping boogers bare-handed, nearly residing in your car, and rarely purchasing anything for yourself.

You're also a woman. And although you may not be able to pursue all of your own interests while in the throes of motherhood, it's important to find little things here and there that are just for you.

The stories in this book are intended to be just that.

They're short. They're hot.
They're a little something just for <u>you</u>.

Enjoy!

What Comes Naturally

Julianna Darling

Veronica Worthington wanted nothing more than something tall, dark, and steaming hot. Her appetite was voracious, and she was ready to gulp it all in, savoring every last drop of its delicious saltiness.

As she neared the front of the line at iBrew, the neighborhood coffee house, she had only one thing on her mind: a salted caramel mocha latte. Tall, dark, and sweet. She was fumbling for her debit card when she heard a familiar voice slide warmly over her skin, sending goose bumps racing down her arms and into her fingertips. She grasped the debit card firmly in her hands, and raised her hazel eyes.

"The usual, Mrs. Worthington?" Chad's mouth turned up in the most delicious way at the corners, half naughty smirk, half sincere schoolboy. His cerulean blue eyes fixated on her lips as he asked.

Flustered, Veronica dropped her debit card on the floor, her cheeks turning rosier by the second. *Holy hell, what is wrong with me?* she silently admonished herself. At thirty-five, and a mother of two, she knew better than to flirt with a college-aged barista. She laughed softly, prepared to stand and face him like the hard-nosed newspaper editor that she was. She chewed up and spit out men hotter than this every day for work. So why did Chad have her so thrown?

Just as she was regaining her composure, Chad's large, firm hand scooped in and picked up her debit card for her, his other hand steadying her back so she wouldn't lose her balance.

Sparks shot through every nerve in her body as he placed the card in her palm, slowly curling one finger at a time over the card to secure it. He held his fingers a beat too long on her fisted hand, covering it warmly in his.

Veronica glanced up, taking in every inch of Chad's body as they rose to stand, from his tattered black Chucks, past his firm thighs, up his flat stomach and over his muscled chest, until, finally, they skated over the stubble riding his chiseled jawline that looked way too mature for a college boy. This time, the blood that rushed to her cheeks just a moment ago shot straight to her stomach, knotting, burning hot between her legs.

"Mrs. Worthington, are you okay?" Chad whispered. "Can I get you some water? You look a little hot today." He smiled crookedly, running his hand along her arm and up to her elbow. As their eyes connected, she realized her heart was beating a little too fast. Perhaps coffee wasn't the best choice today. *What in the world is wrong with me?*

Veronica took a deep breath and smiled, letting it fully reach her eyes. She hadn't received her performing arts major at Bloomsburg University for nothing. She had acted her way through college and bluffed her way into journalism; surely, she could mask the lust racing up her thighs, flashing in her chest, and sending shocks to the very ends of her nipples. *He's a college boy, for God's sake! Get a grip, Veronica!*

"Thank you, Chad. I'm fine, really. Just a clumsy moment—whoops! Butterfingers," she chuckled nervously. *Did I really just say, Whoops! Butterfingers? Shoot me now.*

"Here, it's on me today." He lifted the hot cup of steaming coffee and slowly slid it into a cardboard sleeve, his eyes never leaving hers. "Say—do you have a minute? I was wondering if I could talk to you about an internship at the paper. I'm a writing major at Bloomsburg U and I'd really like to get my foot in the door at the Bloomsburg Weekly. What are my odds of sleeping my way to the top?" He raised his eyebrows, and then laughed when he saw her cheeks stain red for the second time. "Sorry, Mrs. Worthington, I was just kidding, of course."

Veronica took her foot out of her mouth long enough to put her game face on and stop acting like a simpering school girl. "Oh...of course you were." She swatted at his arm, but her hand

8

stopped short when it brushed against the firm ridge of his tricep, taking in the texture of his sinewy hardness. "I'd love to talk to you outside of work some time; we have several internship programs at the paper. I know the boss personally, and she's dynamite," Veronica said, winking at Chad. "How about we meet for lunch tomorrow? The office is closed for the weekend, but unfortunately, an editor's work is never done. Come by and we can chat about your...um, credentials. Though, just know that sleeping your way to the top will only get you so far. You need some game to back up your swagger."

"Oh, I've got game, Mrs. Worthington—"

She interrupted, "Please, call me Veronica. I'm thirty-five, not sixty-five. Mrs. Worthington is my ex mother-in-law. I'm Veronica," she said, finally releasing her hand from the warmth of his arm, her hand feeling naked and empty without the feel of him beneath her fingertips.

"Veronica, I like that. Reminds me of a beach bunny," Chad said, never wavering his gaze. "Why don't I grab some sandwiches and tea from Barney's, make the day easier for you. I'll head over there around one, after my shift ends here. Does that work? I really appreciate this opportunity to talk with you alone about my...qualifications, Mrs. Worth—" he caught himself and continued, "Veronica. I promise, you won't be disappointed."

Despite his easy flirtation and the words that slid from the sensuous curves of his lips—that Veronica suddenly wanted to bite into, while grabbing handfuls of his shaggy blond curls—his eyes were full of excitement for the job opportunity, the desire gone. Had she imagined it? Veronica suddenly felt like a middle-aged fool.

Chad could have his pick of college girls; what would he see in a thirty-five-year-old woman, other than a stepping stone for his career? As if on cue, the little brass bell over iBrew's front door jangled, and in walked a high-chested, perky-eyed blonde. She bee-lined straight for Chad.

"Hey, Chad, when do you get off..." she winked at him, never even glancing at Veronica. "I mean, when do you get off from work? You joining us for senior cram? I wanted to save you a seat next to me, if you want to come..." Blondie twirled one of her long, errant curls around her pointer finger, flashing her dusky blue eyes up at Chad from under waves of long black eyelashes. They fluttered up and down as she bit her lower lip and stared into Chad's eyes.

Hell, she could charm the pants off me! Veronica marveled. How could Chad resist a little nymph like this? Blondie was taller by a good two inches over Veronica's petite five-feet-four-inch frame; the girl's legs seemed to never end, stretching from the frayed edges of her too-short jean shorts with the pockets dangling from beneath the hemline, to the tips of her Rainbow sandals, ten perfectly painted teal nails peeking out. Not to mention that the girl didn't have a bra on, and Veronica could see the dark outline of her high, pointy nipples through the white tank top she was wearing. They were tiny, having never been stretched from breastfeeding. Veronica rolled her eyes, defeated. Who was she kidding?

"Thanks for the coffee, Chad. I've gotta run. Are we still on for tomorrow? I see a lot of potential in you, you'll fit in just fine," Veronica said, glancing toward Blondie with a smug smile on her face. She may not have high, perky nipples any more, but she had something the college girl didn't: power. And she knew how to work it.

*****

Veronica left iBrew in a happier frame of mind than when she'd entered it. She knew she shouldn't be shamelessly flirting with a kid who was a good fifteen years younger than she was, but, hey...it boosted her ego and was just for fun. Lately, Veronica had forgotten how to have fun. Between their subscription numbers plummeting at the paper, her inability to figure out what to do with the kids over summer break, and her nasty arguments with her ex over visitation rights, Veronica was tired. Which was how she found herself at iBrew most mornings these days, casually flirting with a twenty-something-year-old barista. God, her ex would have a fit. Screw him. The reason he was her ex was because he couldn't keep it in his pants long enough to give her a chance to lose her baby weight after their second daughter, Camille, was born.

She'd hardly gotten out of her maternity bras when she'd found the first sext message: Thinking of you makes me wet all over again. Thinking about it now, embarrassment and anger boiled within Veronica, just as it had when she first saw the message. *Did I read that right?* she'd thought incredulously. She'd waited a week and then slipped into her husband's home office while he slept and scrolled through all of his texts until she found what she was looking for.

Angie: What's big & hard & smooth all over?

Dean: It'd better be me u nasty little minx.

Angie: Better. I just installed a pole at the house. Come for a spin!

Dean: Can't. Wife's working late. At home w kids. Tomorrow?

Dean: Then I'll show you what's big & hard & smooth all over.

Angie: Can't wait, babe. I've missed that cock of yours. I'll think of u filling me all night long.

Dean: Damn, girl. Now I'm never gonna sleep. I wish I was there to slide my fingers inside u.

Angie: Can't u find a sitter for an hour? The Viper will never know.

Dean: I wish. I'd much rather be tasting u right now. Mmm...

Veronica had dropped the phone to the desk, her hands shaking. Of all the dirty things she'd read, she was most hurt that the marriage-wrecking slut had called her a viper. And Dean hadn't even defended her. Instead, he'd talked about tasting that bitch. He hadn't done that with Veronica since before the kids were born. She couldn't stop the hot tears as they slipped down her cheeks. She felt like a fool then, and she felt like a fool now.

Snapping herself back to the present, Veronica decided that she would keep their lunch professional; she would talk to Chad about their internship program, and maybe, just maybe, he could help her figure out their online presence to offset their loss of paper subscribers. With a task in mind to keep her thoughts preoccupied—and off Chad's lips—Veronica hurried into the office, a new spring in her step.

*****

That night after work, Veronica picked the kids up from their after school and daycare programs, smiling from ear to ear as she listened to their silly giggles and exuberant notes as they sang off-key to The Lorax. "I'm just doing what comes naturally," Veronica sang along, laughing.

She swung by the Burrito Barn, grabbing take-out to speed up the night. Veronica had spent the day thinking about Chad, imaging every possible dirty scenario she could run him through at the office, and was a little hot and bothered as a result. She glanced in the rear-view mirror at her precious girls. She couldn't change what an asshole their father was, and she'd never give them up for the world. But she wasn't dead. And her ego had taken a hit. She could use Chad as fantasy candy all she wanted. No harm in having a face to picture while she got herself off tonight. Veronica hoped that if she could release some of her pent up heat, then perhaps she could control herself over lunch the next day.

The moment she got the kids to bed, she turned off all the lights for the night and crept back to her first floor master suite. She made sure to lock her bedroom door before she headed into her closet where she kept her secret stash of pleasure toys. She missed the feeling of a real man. It felt as if she and Dean had been together only twice in the last few years of their marriage: once for Brighton and once for Camille. She knew that wasn't true, but she could no longer remember the scent of him, the way his cock was shaped. She couldn't feel the warmth of his lips or remember the way his mouth tasted when covering hers. Their seven-year marriage had given her three things: Brighton, Camille, and a raging desire that was completely unfulfilled. Her broken heart wasn't easy to mend; it had frozen as she went through months and months of reading his sexts with Angie, taking pictures of each screen shot for evidence against him. But there was no glee when the divorce was finally granted.

She felt like a failure, a dried up prune that no one wanted. What had happened to the hot vixen she used to be, who seduced Dean the first week on their college campus? He'd been her acting professor that first year. And though he was the acting

12

master, she later discovered, it was Veronica who had bravely seduced him within the first week of class. It wasn't long before kisses and cuddles led to more. Fingers slipping quickly beneath her skirt after class, a hand-job behind the stage during intermission, hidden by mounds of unused stage props, the crowd's coughs and laughter echoing throughout the auditorium.

She wasn't sure where it went wrong, but Veronica knew one thing. That wild, adventurous girl was still in there. And maybe she'd bring her out to play with Chad.

*****

Veronica dressed carefully the next day. She'd shaved and waxed to perfection the night before, after spending an hour watching erotic videos and imaging Chad's head pushed between her legs as she sat on her desk, her legs dangling over his shoulders. It hadn't taken long for her to bring herself to climax as she twisted in her sheets and soared under the electric buzz that rode against her clit.

She rubbed lotion all over her body, pausing to take stock in her bathroom mirror. For thirty-five, she wasn't half bad. Hell, she was a looker if she really acknowledged the truth. Her long, chestnut-colored hair hung over her toned legs as she bent to massage them with lotion. She stood tall, holding her C-cup breasts in her hands, fuller now after her kids were born, and her dark brown nipples tightened at her touch, creating hard buttons of sensation that she just wanted to rub until she was wet. But she couldn't, or she'd be late.

She slid on her black demi bra, gasping at the sensation of the lace scraping across her nipples. She slid her black lacy thong up her legs, snapping the strap between the soft rounds of her butt cheeks, imaging Chad's fingers running over her ass, cupping it as he pulled her in against his hardness. How would she ever be able to have a serious interview with him when all she wanted was to see him naked, to have him pound into her from behind, her face pressed hard against her mahogany desk? She may not be a hot young college girl, but she had experience on her side. She giggled to herself as she gently clipped on her thigh-high stockings. Chad would not know what hit him, she relished, the inner folds of her lips growing wet at the thought of him running his hand up her stockinged leg until they discovered bare skin secretly tucked away.

God! She was behaving like a tramp and not a businesswoman. Not a mother. Veronica sighed. Was she fooling herself? She wouldn't want to embarrass either of them if they were not on the same page with their desire. Not to mention, she could be fired.

She quickly zipped the back of her pencil skirt and pulled on her jacket before she headed out of her bedroom to get the kids ready for a long weekend at their father's house.

*****

Veronica made it to the office in record time after dropping the kids off with Dean. Dickhead had been standing at the door in his boxer shorts and a terrycloth bathrobe, open, his dark brown hair casually mussed. And damn if he didn't still have the boyish charm she'd fallen in love with. He waved from the door, but Veronica just walked around to the passenger side of her SUV. Brighton tumbled out and ran quickly to her father, hugging him before slipping inside. As Veronica struggled with Camille's car seat straps, she could feel Dean's eyes on her from behind.

She "accidentally" dropped Camille's Sippy cup and bent from the waist, her pencil skirt riding up to reveal the lacy tops of her thigh-high hose. She glanced through her hair, which had tumbled down along the side of her face, and saw Dean gaping from the front porch, coffee spilling from his cup that was now askew in his hand.

Take that, dirt bag, Veronica laughed to herself. She parted her legs ever so slightly, jutting her ass in the air a little higher, before flipping her hair back and righting herself, never once looking Dean's way. She pulled her skirt discreetly over the lace and lifted Camille from the car, laughing on the inside at the hard-on Dean would have to ignore this morning.

*****

The office was empty when Veronica arrived. She'd already popped into iBrew for her regular blend, confirming with Chad that their date...er, their interview...was still on. She'd seen the way his eyes lingered along the deep scoop of her silky violet-colored tank that she wore beneath her blazer. Her silver necklace glistened just between the curves of her breasts.

She filled the morning with busy work to keep her mind off of Chad. The few people who had come in to help prep the paper for printing were long gone. Veronica was leaning over her desk, filing some paperwork into separate folders when she sensed Chad walking in. It wasn't just the rustle of their bagged lunch that caught her ear; all of her senses were heightened and drawn to the pure masculine energy he exuded. For someone so young, he carried himself with the confidence of a seasoned lover.

"Mrs. Worthington, your lunch is here," Chad murmured from the doorway.

Veronica never even turned around. She thought of this morning's performance for Dean and bent over a little further, baring the top of her lace stocking once again, praying it ignited the same effect as it had on her ex-husband. She wasn't disappointed. From across the room, she could hear Chad swallow hard as he asked, "Would you like me to close your office door, Veronica?"

"Please," she said huskily, turning her head over her shoulder so their eyes met. The minute they did, they locked, and she knew it was game on. She winked and said, "I'll be right with you. I just have a few files I need to tuck away. The first rule of a successful paper is an efficient editor, one who knows just where to put things, how to move things around to fit. Wouldn't you agree, Chad?" She bent down a fraction further and felt the rustle of lace against cotton as her pencil skirt rode up even more, revealing the clip of her garter.

She waited for Chad to move. In that tense moment of electricity, she wondered if she'd made an error. Perhaps she'd misread the desire in his eyes earlier? She heard the door slowly close, and then the barely audible click as Chad locked it behind him. She waited patiently, her panties getting wet as she heard

15

Chad drop their lunch on the table and cross the room, the thighs of his jeans rubbing together as he closed the gap between them.

"Veronica, do you think you could teach me everything you know? I want to rise to the top of this field," he said, as he placed his left hand on the side of her hip, sending shock waves to her toes. She shuddered, feeling a wave of desire flash between her legs. She backed up slightly, pressing her hip into his hand, until her butt hit its target and brushed his leg as she stood. She turned slightly, their eyes meeting.

"Are you sure you're ready to learn? If you're going to be my protégé, you need to work very hard and show me what you're made of. Do you think you can do that?" Her eyes stayed on his, despite her confidence faltering in their little charade. She thought of Blondie and Angie, and heaved her chest higher, determined not to let them get the best of her. She was long overdue for some fun and games, and Chad was just the right partner. She turned to face him, slapping the file down hard against the desk.

"I won't have insubordinate interns, do you understand me?" She saw the desire flash within Chad's irises, growing intense and dark. He licked his lips and nodded, his hand digging deeper into her hip. He yanked her an inch forward, heat searing through the lower part of her tummy as he did. She swallowed, placing her hand against his chest. "Chad, there's one other thing about this paper."

"Yeah?" he barely got out, running his hand lower down her thigh, tracing it along the hemline of her skirt. "What's that Veronica?" He leaned in and inhaled her clean, flowery scent. "What is that scent? It's driving me mad." He leaned forward and buried his nose in her neck, tracing it up to the edge of her jaw, never once using his tongue or his lips. The sensation was driving Veronica crazy.

"We always have to deliver. Can you promise me that?" Veronica bit her lip and lowered her hand between Chad's legs. She could feel his hardness through his jeans, eager to be free in her hand. She ran her palm up and down the fabric, teasing him ever so lightly.

"Veronica," he gasped, closing in and dropping his mouth to hers.

16

His kiss sent fireworks through her tummy as the warmth of his lips surrounded hers, taking, demanding, confident. He tugged her bottom lip through his teeth, shooting stars to the wetness of her thighs.

"What does the boss have in mind for me today?" Chad asked, his fingers finding the bare flesh of her thigh. "God, your skin is so smooth. You are so beautiful, do you know that?" Their tongues rolled together, as his fingers slid lazily along the lace, around her thigh, and between her legs until, finally, they found their home. He groaned when he touched the bottom of her panties and felt how wet they already were.

His tongue drove deeper into Veronica's mouth as she tugged at Chad's jeans, opening the button and trying to lower his pants. Without breaking their kiss, she heard him tease, "Eh-eh-eh," as he shook his head no and slid two fingers deeply inside her, pushing higher and higher until Veronica thought she would explode. Wave after wave crested over her as he expertly maneuvered his fingers within her, grazing her g-spot until she shook and tightened around his fingers. He pulled them from within her and brought them to his lips, inhaling her scent. He licked them, sucking greedily, as his gaze bore into her bewitching hazel eyes, almost green from desire.

She turned so Chad could unzip her skirt, letting it drop to the floor. She heard him gasp when he saw the thong riding between her cheeks. His palm smacked her backside and rubbed it vigorously, as he stroked the outline of his cock with his other hand. She knew she was pushing him too far, and she loved every second of it. She slipped her tank over her head and turned to face him, her breasts filling the revealing demi bra. He bent his head and tugged a nipple free with his teeth, drawing it into his mouth and sucking hard, causing her to gasp. Dean had never spent much time on her breasts, so this brought a whole new level of sensation tugging on her nether lips. He bit down hard, rolling his tongue around the base of her nipple. She couldn't hold back the moan as she grabbed fistfuls of his blond curls and called out, "Chad! Oh, God..." She felt her body convulse again as a mini orgasm shook her senses. She removed her bra and stood there in just her thong, garter, and spiked heels. When Chad pulled her in for a deep kiss, she never wanted it to end.

17

Nearly delirious from pleasure, she dropped to her knees and freed Chad of his pants, finally, yanking down his boxers with her teeth, then hands. The wide, long girth of him spilled out and she nearly gasped at his full size. She'd never been with a man this large before, but her insides were on fire as she imagined him moving within her. She wrapped her hands around his shaft, rubbing it until he grew larger still. Her lips closed around the tip of his erection as she slid his hard, long length deeply inside her mouth. Dear God, the taste of him made her greedy. She sucked vigorously as she felt his hand grab the back of her head, his hands laced within her hair.

He groaned, "Veronica, you're gonna make me come before I can really deliver. Come up here, woman, I want all of you."

Veronica's lips took one last stroke of his length and then she rose on her tiptoes, staring into his deep blue eyes. Her arms wrapped around his waist, his hardness pressing against her stomach with a dangerous heat. They both stood there for a moment, chests heaving, on the brink of madness.

She heard the tear of a wrapper and Chad slid a condom on, his eyes never leaving hers. Before she knew what was happening, he flipped her around and bent her over the desk. He placed one hand firmly on her shoulder, and with the other hand, he gently moved her thong to the side, making way for something larger. He slid his fingers inside the wet slit between her legs, opening her moistened lips to fit his cock.

Veronica gasped when he slid in his full, wide length, pushing it deeper inside, deeper still, until he bottomed out against her backside. He paused for a moment, kissing her neck, her back, her jawline, turning her head and kissing her from behind as he cupped her breasts, tweaking her hard nipples. Reflexively, she backed against him, rocking, wanting to be taken. Before she knew what was happening, she heard, "Chad, fuck me," come from her own lips, and she realized how badly she wanted it. "God, fuck me, now!" she demanded.

"Yes, ma'am," Chad growled, yanking her head back with a fistful of hair, pulling on it, causing her to tighten around his cock.

18

He started thrusting inside of her, holding her hip with his other hand, slamming against her as his length slid in and out, pumping faster and harder. Veronica was lost in desire as he rode her this way, over and over, until wave after wave of orgasm shook her body. Without pulling out, he turned her over on the desk, dragging her legs over his shoulders, driving himself even deeper. She met his eyes, facing his passion head on. His face was young, but the heat in his eyes was all for her. He was lost in intense pleasure because of her. The thought drove her wild and she arched her hips to meet his, beat for beat. His fingers found her clit as he slid, wet and slippery in and out of her, making her writhe beneath his hands and the width of his cock. She wasn't sure she could take much more as she arched and came once again.

Her wet insides clenched around him, causing him to explode, and he leaned down and took her mouth, riding out his orgasm and shaking with each drop of his pleasure.

Chad rested his head on Veronica's chest, gently, softly kissing her nipples. Veronica sighed, running her fingers through his hair, luxuriating in the new feeling washing over her: sexual power. For the first time in a good long while, Veronica felt her power again. More than just making Chad come, she'd needed to feel desired again, and she did; he'd worshipped her body as no one ever had before. He may be young, but he was her ticket to finding herself again. To soak in the life of passion she wanted to live. In that moment, she knew she would be okay, after all was said and done.

But she wasn't ready for it to end just yet. Veronica began to laugh, her back sticking to the desk, wet from their enthusiastic session. She looked up at Chad, meeting his eyes and seeing his desire riding strong again, for her. It made her heady.

"Veronica—" he started. But she interrupted, ready to take control of her life.

"Chad, you're definitely hired!"

They both laughed, until their eyes met again, and his lips fell back onto hers, slowly, slowly, as he began moving again within her.

Beheld

Shenoa Carroll-Bradd

"Don't," she whispered.

My hands stopped just beneath her breasts. "What's wrong?"

"Nothing, I just...you don't want to touch me there."

I felt a smile tug at my cheeks, but halted its spread. The last thing I wanted was for Hannah to think I was laughing at her. "Trust me though. I really do. Don't you want me to?"

Her breath sounded unsteady.

I liked the tremulous sound, but wished that I was the cause of her quickening pulse, not her insecurity.

"Yes," she said. "Yes of course I want you to. I just don't want to gross you out."

Again, I had to focus on not smiling. "Sweetheart..."

"No, don't use that voice. It's easy for you to say you want to be with me, when you haven't seen...all of me." She was quiet for a moment. "There's a lot of me Tyson, and none of it's pretty."

I shook my head, then reach a hand up for her cheek.

Hannah obligingly guided me.

"What you're telling me is utter gibberish." I leaned in and kissed her, softly, not pressing. I recognized the quaver in her voice. I knew how vulnerable she was in that moment, and though I ached for her, I refused to further the damage already done by years of doubt, judgment, and ignorance. "Maybe I haven't seen you," I allowed, "but don't believe for a second that that means I can't *perceive* you." My fingers stroked her cheek, her chin, her lips. "You say you're not pretty..."

"I don't just say, I know." Her voice rose, threatening tears if I didn't tread carefully.

"Let me tell you what I know." I pressed her shoulder gently until she lay back, and I swung a cautious leg over, straddling her hips. I could feel the heat of her, but that could wait. That *had* to wait, until I could show her how I truly saw her. I leaned forward in the overly-dim room, and found her face again. "I know that your cheeks are soft, like sun-warmed peaches, and that when you hug me, the touch of them is just as comforting as the wrap of your arms."

"They're jowly," she interjected.

I slid my thumb over her lips. "That's what you think, my dear. I'm telling you what I *know*." I traced the curve of her lips with the pad of my thumb, back and forth, feeling her start to smile beneath my touch. "I know that your lips are the sweetest I've ever kissed."

Her jaw tensed and her lips parted, ready to launch another denial.

I blocked the negativity with a kiss.

"No arguing," I said. "Just listen. Your lips remind me of a rose garden my grandmother tended when I was a boy. She would take me by the hand," I raised Hannah's hand to my lips as I spoke, so she could feel the flow of my breath and the rhythm of my words while I continued tracing the outline of her lips, "and lead me to the best blooms. She held the stems for me so I wouldn't accidentally grab a thorn, and I used to lean in and smell them, putting my face close against the blossoms, sticking my nose right in the center and letting the velvet petals tickle my face. And that's how your lips feel to me, Hannah. Soft, and sweet, and magical as rose petals. I don't care if you think they're the wrong color or shape, too plump or too thin. I just know they're the sweetest I've ever tasted, and they make me smile." I could feel her smiling too. I kissed her fingertips one by one, then laid her hand back on her bare stomach, trailing my own hand upward, easing toward her chest.

She tensed.

"I know that all breasts are different," I said, cupping her left breast in my right hand, feeling the weight of it, the supple give beneath my fingers. "And I've never cared if they happen to

21

be shy A cups or overflowing D's." I massaged her, rubbing her nipple gently back and forth between my thumb and forefinger. "I know that there's magic in each one, though. The magic of youth, the magic of sustenance, and often just the magic of joy. I love the way they bounce, and the sight of them jiggling is what I imagine heaven must be like."

She giggled quietly, which was good, because this next part was going to be difficult.

"And I know that I don't care how many breasts a woman has either."

Hannah went silent.

"I mean, how can I judge? I have none." I meant it as a joke, but she was not laughing. I gently placed my left hand below the mastectomy scar that crossed her chest from sternum to armpit.

Hannah pulled in a shaky breath.

"I know that you don't like your scar," I said softly, not wanting to spook her. "But it is a part of you. I love it, and would like to touch it."

I gave her a moment to absorb my words.

"May I touch your scar, Hannah?"

Her voice, when it came, was shaky and damp. "Yes," she said, and nothing else.

I moved slowly, smoothing my hand up her chest, over the flat plane where a breast once stood, where her children, now grown, once suckled. When my fingers reached that puckered ribbon, she sucked in a breath through her teeth. I feared she might change her mind, but she didn't.

Hannah stayed quiet, letting me run two fingers back and forth over the scar, as I had done with her lips.

As my left hand explored, my right continued massaging her remaining breast, tempering her fear and insecurity with the comfort of contact and the burgeoning glow of pleasure.

"We all have scars," I told her, feeling her chest hitch beneath my hands. "And they tell our stories. When I feel this," I bent over and pressed my lips softly to her scar, the part of herself she hated most, "I feel your strength. I feel a banner that proclaims 'Cancer raised its ugly head, and I told it no.'" I nuzzled the scar with my cheek, hearing her heartbeat, her quiet

22

breaths. "I know that there should be no shame in turning away a monster. No guilt in battle scars. This part of you will never be ugly to me, Hannah. This scar fills me with gratitude that a woman so full of strength, determination, and life, could find something of equal worth inside of me."

I scooted back, placing a hand on the stomach that she swore sagged, that she said was striped with scars and stretch marks. It felt so soft, so warm and comforting beneath my hand. I placed a kiss above her navel, smelling the light scent of her skin, the vanilla body wash she used, the coconut lotion she rubbed into her skin after every shower.

"I know that I love your stomach," I told her, "and that if you went under the knife, I would miss whatever part of you the doctors stole away."

I moved farther down, massaging her thighs. "I know that I love your thighs, and that you should too. They're like two strong, fierce lions, guarding the gates of an empress's pleasure garden."

I eased her legs apart, laying kisses along the insides of her thighs, brushing my face against the coarse, springy hair at their juncture. "I know that children have passed through the bones here, and into the world. That does not repel me. That does not make me think your sex is any less wonderful. In fact," I breathed softly on her bare skin, blowing my breath across her thighs, "I find you so much more interesting for it. Yours is a body that has lived, has loved, has been hurt, and has triumphed over the darkness. Your body is a testament to the human spirit, and I will not let you speak ill against it."

I rested my cheek against her left thigh and softly stroked her pubic hair as if it were a beloved cat. "The world may say hateful, stupid things, but I won't. And you won't."

With my fingertips, I sought her out, feeling her heat, her slick wetness, caressing her beauty until she began to shudder.

"And in this relationship, as far as I can see, ours are the only relevant opinions. I would tell you my thoughts on your shins, your ankles, your feet and toes, but I think you get my point. I think...I *hope* you're starting to glimpse how I really see you, Hannah."

I lowered my face to her, bathed in the warm, musky, unique scent, feeling her heat, tasting the salty tang as she came alive on my tongue.

Hannah moaned and arched her back.

After a moment, I lifted my head. "You've stayed very quiet. How do you feel about all this? What I've said?"

Her voice still carried the raw edge of recent tears, but through that poured the dawning glow of joy. "I feel...beautiful," she said.

I smiled, and lowered my lips to her once more.

Time For Indulgence

Lizzie Richards

It was her secret. She didn't need to tell anyone about it—not where she was going, what she was doing, or who she was meeting. Not that anyone asked. As soon as anyone found out she was a single mother with no partner, the assumption came that she had no life outside of her children. She would smile and laugh and admit that yes, they did take up a lot of her time, but it was time gladly given. Being a mother was a large part of who she was—a defining role—but it was not *all* she was. As much as she put aside her own needs for those of her children, there were also things she needed to do for herself and times when she needed to put herself first. Sharon did not wish to live a celibate life, nor did she see why she should have to.

One evening, a commercial for a dating site appeared when she was flicking through the channels, searching for some mindless program she could keep on in the background while she did the ironing. It had been innocuous enough; happy faces and charming couples extolling the virtues of the particular website, talking about marriage and first dates and perfect matches. She wasn't sure what it was that convinced her to sign up, as she did not want another relationship: the children's father had left a jarring note in her consciousness where reliable men were concerned. She didn't want another man to swoop into her life with promises he would not keep, and she definitely didn't want to expose her children to that.

However, after only a few days on the site, it became apparent that the people there were not the picture-perfect models from the advertisement. While many claimed to want something long-term and meaningful, there were plenty who were only looking for some quick fun. It wasn't long before she received pictures of cocks in her inbox and propositions from guys who were looking for a no strings tumble. Dirty conversations soon developed between them, a taboo that made her insides thrill with each new word typed and sent.

The few hours between finishing her morning at work and picking her children up from school became time she put aside for herself to peruse the site and reply to messages. It was not every day—it couldn't be—but a pattern of regular indulgences emerged. Strange, that she should think of taking time for herself as an indulgence—but that was the difference between living an independent life and one where she had children who relied on her.

She enjoyed talking to these men online and that was fine. Meeting them in person, however, was an entirely different hurdle.

It wasn't something she originally planned to do. She did not know them, and she could not trust them. Warnings bandied around her mind; cautionary tales of men taking advantage, steps to be taken to ensure safety, advice that not all on the Internet are who they claim to be. Yet there was something that appealed to her about the idea of meeting a stranger for sex. Something exciting. When she was younger, she hadn't thought twice about leaving a club with a man she did not know—the difference was that now she had people depending on her. And, that she had met the man online rather than in a crowded, dimly-lit room. Part of her mind told her she should feel dirty for doing it, that she should be ashamed; but the rest of her knew it was no different than what she had done before, and she knew she should not be ashamed of her sexuality.

So it was that Sharon walked the short distance from where she parked her car to the budget hotel just off the main street. It was the safest place she could think of: plenty of staff, semi-public, neutral ground. She refused to take a strange man back to her house and would not follow one back to his. She had pre-paid for the room online with her credit card, a solid piece of evidence should she go missing. She had to leave by a set time, or her children would not be collected from school and her absence would be noted. The only precaution she didn't take was telling someone where she was going, but she knew that she couldn't. Despite how far women's rights had come, the stigma of seeking and having casual sex would reach her, and her competency as a mother might even be questioned because of it. She couldn't risk that.

She had planned to get dressed up before the encounter, to make it seem like a romantic tryst so common in the novels she read, but instead her meeting that morning had dragged on and on. She hadn't had time to change and her fancy underwear was scrunched in the bottom of her bag, trapped beneath misshapen sandwiches. The slightly sweaty blouse and trousers she already wore would have to do—she did not feel sexy, but she supposed that even if she had prepared herself thoroughly, she would still experience the intense nerves that made her stomach wobble.

They had arranged to meet in the bar. Walking toward it, she felt sick. She flirted with the idea of leaving, of going home and forgetting the day; but curiosity pressed her forward. Her accidental tardiness proved a blessing, as it gave her an excuse to look at the man she was meeting from an unobserved distance.

He was the only person at the bar, instantly recognizable from his photo. With short, dark hair thinning at the temples, and a slim figure clad in a suit with long legs curled under the bar stool, he was as handsome and well-groomed as he had appeared online.

She dithered. What if he took one look at her aging body and backed out? She knew her stomach had become more rounded, fading stretch marks littering both it and her untoned thighs. Her breasts would droop as soon as they were free of her bra. She was not dressed to impress, and looked all of her years. *Sharon,* she reminded herself, *if he wanted a younger woman, he would have propositioned one.* But he had not. He had come to her.

The slight crinkling around his eyes when he smiled at her approach sent butterflies through her stomach. Her self worth was not based entirely on others' opinions, but she would be lying if she didn't admit that knowing she was still desirable gave her a boost of confidence.

"Sorry I'm late," she said, as she took a seat next to him. "You must be Mark?"

"I was beginning to think you'd gotten cold feet." His voice was deeper than she had expected, a rough baritone that seemed to vibrate through her. "I'm glad you didn't. You're much more beautiful in person." He pressed a kiss to her cheek, one that lingered slightly longer than for a simple greeting. His cleanly shaven skin was soft against hers, the spicy cologne he wore hitting the right tone within her as his words made her blush.

"Can I get you anything?" the bartender asked.

"No, we'll be going up to our..."

"A lime and tonic, please," she cut Mark off, then threw him an apologetic smile.

"Have you done this before?"

Unsure whether to tell the truth or lie, she hesitated, which seemed to give him all the answer he needed.

"It's okay, I'll go easy on you." He winked, just as his hand landed on her thigh and gave it what she assumed was meant to be a reassuring squeeze. She looked down at it, noting how long his fingers were, and an involuntary shudder of anticipation ran through her.

"So, how..." she began.

His lips met hers in a sudden kiss, a surprised noise escaping her lips as she felt his hand travel further upward. She gripped it with hers to stop it, and broke the kiss with a slight gasp.

"Not here."

"We can take the drinks up to the room," Mark said, before he stood and collected both glasses. Sharon nodded and followed him, taking note of how his suit clung to his ass as he walked, his strides long and purposeful. He had gone a little soft around the middle, but who had not at their age? She knew she certainly was not as trim as she had once been, especially after bearing children. But they were going to her room. He wanted her, couldn't wait to have her, found her sexually attractive despite her flaws, and that was a heady compliment.

The short elevator ride to the third floor was taken in tense silence. Sharon fidgeted with the key card to the room, her eyes fixed on the little screen that showed the floor number. A hand placed on her lower back made her breath hitch in surprise. She could feel him watching her even as she tried to ignore it and focus on her breathing instead; her nerves would calm down soon enough. She hoped.

As soon as she locked the door to the hotel room, Mark pressed her into the wall, his mouth hot and demanding as his tongue probed her with the taste of bitter ale. Her bag dropped with a dull thump as she reached to touch and undress him. His jacket was thrown to the floor without care and she clung to his shirt, almost on tiptoes as she craned her head up to reach him, her hands wandering and groping until they found his ass. She tilted her hips to his and pulled him closer, smiling into the kiss with satisfaction as she felt his cock begin to harden against her stomach.

"I've only got until two-thirty," she said in a gasp when he began to kiss down her neck, unbuttoning her blouse as he went.

"Got to get back to your husband?" He smirked as he looked at her before continuing his trail.

"It's not...I don't have..."

"Don't worry," he said. "We'll just have to make this round count."

Flutters of excitement flew through her stomach as he slid her blouse from her shoulders, his mouth seeking out the newly exposed skin, his throaty noises of desire rumbling against her. He fondled her breasts through the plain fabric of her bra, the sensations muted but delightful nonetheless. Clever fingers sought their way inside a cup to brush against a nipple, making her gasp as he pinched and caressed, his lips peppering kisses across her modest cleavage.

A contorted twist and a self-conscious laugh had him stepping back as she reached behind herself to unclasp her bra, the hook so simple to undo on her own now proving problematic for her shaking fingers.

"Let me," he offered, capturing her mouth in a kiss once more as he reached to help her. Each brush of his fingers against her skin seemed purposeful, making the act feel more intimate and less clumsy. Soon it was unclasped, his deft hands working quickly to rid her of her blouse and bra as she leaned back against the wall.

He paused to smile down at her, his hands trailing along her bared skin in a light, appreciative touch that made her shiver.

"Gorgeous," he muttered, before he bent again to kiss her breasts. He reached into her slacks as he sucked a nipple into his mouth, his tongue teasing and gentle as he rubbed against her core through her panties, his fingers sure and firm as they urged her to rock against them.

Sharon let out a short, breathy moan as she shifted against his hand, her arousal seeping through the cloth to dampen his fingers. A nick of teeth against her nipple made her gasp before his mouth returned to hers. She pulled off his shirt as she kissed him, keeping his lips on hers in a passionate kiss as she felt her pleasure rise. He moved her panties aside to allow his fingers to part her slick folds, offering more friction and rubbing smoothly over her clit. She let her head fall back, eyes closed against the sensation, the wall gratefully solid as he rubbed her with the soft pads of his fingers, stroking across her nub rhythmically to tease and excite.

"I want you." Her voice was strained, breathless.

"Condom?"

"In my bag."

He released her to shrug the rest of the way out of his shirt, backing off to give her enough space to look through her bag. She let out an embarrassed huff as she wrestled with its contents while sneaking glances to where Mark was removing his belt. A triumphant grin accompanied her to the bed after she fished the shiny packets from her bag's depths, discarding her shoes along the way.

Wriggling out of her slacks and panties, she paused with a soft gasp after turning to fully look at Mark.

He was standing at the foot of the bed, watching her as he stroked his erection, now free of its confines as his trousers hung open and hugged his thighs. He looked so confident and sure, his hand moving in smooth strokes as his eyes roamed over Sharon's body. He was appreciating her, was aroused by her—and it made her feel fantastic.

She climbed onto the bed, one of the packets clutched in her hand as she crawled toward him. She urged him to come closer until his knees pressed against the mattress, allowing her easy access without strain. She took her time stroking up his thighs and kissing at his skin, inhaling the musky scent of a morning of work in a woollen suit. She carefully rolled the condom onto his cock, stroking him as she did so, before nuzzling against the wiry curls at its base. She had missed the scent and feel of a man, and so she reveled in it.

He pushed her back and she let herself fall to the mattress with a light thump, one arm immediately reaching to grasp his back as he shifted on top of her. He framed her with his arms as she guided him in with her other hand, her leg hooked over his and tangled in his trousers, tilting her hips to meet his as he thrust. Her fingers wandered to her clit, massaging it in time with his movements.

An involuntary grin spread across her face as he moved. He felt so good, his cock hard and insistent inside her, his mouth at her neck, his breath hot on her skin and sending prickles of warmth through her body with each grunt. She tingled with pleasure, her back arched and stomach tightened with each rock of her hips to encourage him deeper. He lacked style and finesse but he more than made up for it in effort, gripping her hips tightly and pulling her further onto his cock with each thrust, the slapping of skin loud in the small room, the squelching sound they made with every movement making her blush, but also causing excitement as he moaned about her wetness being so hot and all for him.

He came with a shudder and a drawn-out curse, hips stuttering against hers as he held her tightly. She kept her eyes closed, fingers still working her clit even as he pulled out, ignoring his movements as he disposed of the condom. She could feel her climax building, deep within her belly, drawn on by her fingers and encouraged by her other hand, free to pinch at her nipples and make her hum with pleasure as it washed over her, a taut wave that left her feeling pleasantly exhausted and satisfied.

As much as men were useful for penetration, she had learned long ago that the only person she could rely on to successfully bring her to orgasm was herself.

She watched Mark dress while she waited for the buzz to dissipate before getting up to gather her belongings into her bag. A quick check of it ensured everything was still there; a glance at her phone told her that she had enough time for a shower before she had to leave.

"Thank you," she said, and placed a chaste kiss on his lips.

If he had expected her to say anything more he would have been disappointed; instead, she retreated to the bathroom. The heavy creak of the room's door sounded his departure, a dull click shutting him out and leaving her to enjoy her shower in peace. There would be no awkward goodbyes to dance around.

As she stood under the weak and intermittent stream of water, washing the smell and sweat of sex off of her skin, she could not help but smile. The dull ache in her abdomen would serve as a pleasant reminder of the afternoon's activity for a few days, and she could return to her regular life of running around after her children with a renewed spring in her step.

She would definitely have to do this again.

Just Like Old Times

Lori Verni-Fogarsi

Bill stepped through the front door, his computer bag weighing heavily on his shoulder. He'd decided to come home early and do his afternoon meetings over the phone so he would have no problem being home in time to attend their son's high school football game.

He was just about to call out to her when he heard Candace's voice coming from the kitchen.

"Diddle diddle, twat twat, now I found the pussy spot!"

Hysterical laughter came from two voices, and he realized that she had her friend Melody on speaker. They'd been friends since their own high school days and the two would often catch up over the phone, using the speakerphone feature while they each prepared dinner or did other chores.

But "diddle diddle, twat twat?" He knew the girls could get raunchy at times, but he couldn't imagine what that meant, or why they were both laughing like crazy about it. Feeling somewhat guilty, he stood quietly in the entryway, his curiosity getting the better of his knowledge that he was eavesdropping.

"I mean, don't get me wrong," he heard Candace say, "we have a decent sex life, but it's just become so…efficient."

"At least you have orgasms," Melody replied. "I've been faking mine so long I can't remember what it's like to have one with a non battery-operated, live man."

"You really need to stop doing that," Candace said, her tone imparting that this was not the first time they'd discussed it.

"What? And ruin his illusion? You know how I feel about that."

"Chickenshit," Candace said. "Better you than me if you're willing to go your entire life without orgasms."

Melody laughed. "Look who's calling the chicken shit, Mrs. 'it's become so mechanical I could die of boredom!'"

"Touché!"

Bill's heart plummeted as if on a roller coaster. He knew it was just girl talk but he couldn't help feeling insulted; he thought they had a great sex life. Sure, the two or three times a week they made love were pretty much always...the same. But he thought that was one of the comforts of marriage, of knowing one another so well.

"Gotta run, girl. Talk to you soon."

"Me too. Love ya!"

Not wanting to get caught listening, Bill quickly cleared his throat and forced out, "Hey babe, I'm home!" just as the two disconnected.

"Hey, darling, this is a nice surprise," Candace said, walking toward him from the kitchen while wiping her hands on a towel. Her eyes sparkled with pleasure after what he knew had probably been at least an hour catching up with her friend.

Trying to behave normally, he forced a casual tone and said, "Who were you on the phone with? Melody?"

"Um, yeah," she replied, turning back toward the kitchen. "There's still coffee. Want some?"

"No thanks," he said, setting his computer bag on the counter.

She looked at him.

He looked at her.

Deciding to get straight to the point, Candace said, "So, how long have you been standing there listening to us talk?"

Damn! She knew him too well and now he was busted.

"Just a couple of minutes. I didn't want to interrupt."

An uncomfortable pause stood between them, and Candace started busying herself wiping the counter and putting things in the dishwasher.

"Why didn't you just tell me if you think our sex life is boring?"

The two had an excellent marriage overall, their daily interactions resembling those of best friends far more than the

34

stereotypical husband-and-wife-as-near-enemies cliché that seemed to plague so many marriages. Leaving things unspoken was not their style.

Candace sighed. "Please, babe. Don't read more into it than what it was. I wasn't saying our sex life is boring, just that it's kind of the same all the time. Had you been *eavesdropping* earlier, you'd know that we also talked about how you can't expect the sex after fifteen years of marriage to be like it was when you were dating."

He knew she was trying to make him feel better but he actually felt kind of worse. A reminder sounded on his phone: he had to be on a call in five minutes.

"I've got to go set up for my call," he said, lifting his bag.

"Okay, love," she said, walking over and sliding her arms up and around his neck. "But please know that I'm very happy in our marriage and I love our sex life."

"Yeah, yeah. Okay." He gave her a quick kiss, then turned toward his home office, both of them knowing that at the core of things, everything was fine between them.

But still.

*****

The next day was a Saturday and the kids left bright and early in the morning for an overnight trip with their church youth group. They didn't need to be picked up until 6:00 pm on Sunday, and Bill and Candace had already been looking forward to some alone time.

Bill decided to make it better than their typical alone time, which would normally consist of going to the local wine bar for a glass, leaving early because they preferred each other's company to that of strangers, coming home to watch Law & Order on television, then heading up to the bedroom to have *efficient* sex.

He'd wracked his brain trying to think of the best dates they'd had back in the early days; ones that Candace had mentioned over the years. He'd decided on one and found himself fighting hard-ons throughout the day as he planned its re-creation for their Saturday night.

Around noon, when she was out running errands, he sent her a text: *I'm looking forward to dating you tonight.*

Candace, waiting on line at the dry cleaner's, read it with a mixture of guilt and pleasure. On one hand, she was excited that he was apparently planning something. On the other, she was sorry that he'd taken her girl talk so seriously.

She replied: *Really? Where are we going?*

Bill: *Staying home. You don't need to do anything special.*

Candace: *Okaaay (?!) Gotta run. See you later. Xoxoxo*

*****

Arriving home later in the afternoon, Candace was pleasantly surprised to find that Bill had vacuumed, wiped down the bathrooms, and dusted the living room.

"I wanted to make sure you could fully relax tonight," he said by way of explanation. "Even though I always think everything looks clean, I know it bothers you when it's not done."

"Wow, that's really nice. Thank you!" she said, meaning it. She had no illusions about the fact that she was very Type-A, and the truth was, she loved it when the house was clean, especially when the kids weren't home. You could leave a room, come back, and it would still be clean! It was an anomaly she tried to enjoy whenever they weren't around.

By evening time, her excitement had built even further after Bill explained that he had everything planned, she didn't need to do anything dinner-wise, and she should meet him in the living room at 7:00 pm, just like when they were dating and she would come over to his place.

With nothing else to do but relax, she'd taken a long, hot shower, spending extra time to carefully shave her delicate parts, her clitoris already beginning to throb in anticipation. Fighting the urge to stroke herself, she vowed to wait for the evening ahead and instead directed her lust toward doing her hair and makeup to perfection, and choosing an outfit that would be suitable for a living room date while hopefully driving Bill crazy.

Right at 7:00, she walked downstairs to meet him and smiled widely upon instantly recognizing the date he was recreating.

The fireplace was crackling and there was a blanket spread out in front of it with two lap tables, each set with plates, silverware, and water glasses. Bill was unpacking more Chinese food than any two people could ever eat, arranging it neatly on newspapers he'd spread out so the grease wouldn't leak through to the blanket.

Upon seeing her, he stood, lifted a filled wine glass from the side table, and brought it to her. She could tell he was having a hard time looking at her eyes instead of her breasts when he said, "Here you go. I've been looking forward to this all day."

"Me too. Thank you," she said, taking the glass and unlocking their eyes, graciously allowing him to take in the sight of her cleavage.

She was wearing jeans and a low-plunging, short-sleeved sweater that showed more of the creamy curves of her breasts than was decent. It was low enough that she had to wear a special bra with it; one that displayed the girls high and separated, yet without being able to see the bra. She knew that Bill loved the way it looked, but after wearing it out with him once, she'd decided not to anymore because he'd been preoccupied all evening with the attention it brought from other men. While part of her thought that was silly, another part agreed that if you had to wear a special bra, maybe he did have a point.

"You look very…um…sexy," he choked out, drinking in the sight of her.

It had been a long time since she'd elicited that kind of reaction from him and she felt a jolt of excitement trill through her while at the same time recognizing that maybe he wasn't the only one who'd become complacent.

"Are you hungry?" he asked. "Hope so."

He led her over to the blanket and began serving small portions of each of her favorites onto her plate. The stereo was playing in the background, at just the right volume that they were still able to have conversation.

And conversation they had! Bill, being a problem-solving sort of man, had armed himself ahead of time with topics such as

Nickelback's latest tour plans, a new technology controversy that was causing the stock market to fluctuate wildly, and his friend's Good Citizen Award for his abundant service during the Colorado floods.

Appreciative of both the fact that he'd taken the time to come up with things other than the kids to discuss, and that he was so smart and interesting, Candace quickly found herself losing her appetite for Chinese and yearning more and more for Bill.

He stood, taking their wine glasses to go refill them, and she noticed the unmistakable bulge in his pants that meant he was feeling the same way.

During the few moments he was gone, she quickly closed the tops of all the food and set everything aside. He returned with the wine and sat beside her.

"Thank you," she said, leaning in to give him a quick kiss.

He wasn't having quick.

Placing his hand on her cheek, he kept her face close to his as he murmured against her lips, "You're even smarter and more beautiful than when we met."

Breathless, she held still, enjoying the feel of his breath and his words.

He deepened the kiss, but only slightly, running his tongue gently along the edges of her lips, dipping it into her mouth for a moment, but withdrawing it quickly, before her tongue could find his.

She leaned in, trying to find his tongue, to increase the pressure. To kiss like they normally did.

"Shh, baby. Let's take it slow. I want to taste you. We have all night." He continued to tease her lips, sucking them into his mouth, then circling and dipping his tongue inside, causing her nipples to harden and a molten fire to begin smoldering between her legs.

She relaxed, letting herself melt under his kisses, one of her hands roaming over the masculinity of his shoulder and neck, her other hand weakly holding her wine glass.

He broke the kiss to set both their glasses on the side table, then returned to nibbling on her. "You're driving me crazy with that sweater," he said, running his fingertips over the exposed, white mounds. He pulled back, his eyes skating over her with hunger.

She hadn't felt this desirable in years.

Speechless, she placed her hands on each side of his head and brought his face to her chest, where he brushed his face back and forth between the crests, his fingers finding her hard nipples through her sweater and tweaking them rhythmically.

"Mmm," she moaned, reaching for the buttons of his shirt.

He grasped her wrist, stopping her, his eyes telling her that they were not going to do their usual, frenzied, "Wanna fuck? Yes, let's do," routine.

Placing his hand on her shoulder, he laid her back on the blanket and began running his hands over her temples, smoothing her hair back, then continuing down her neck, shoulders, and arms, as his eyes drank her in. Occasionally, he brushed his hands across her still-clothed nipples, making her arch, straining, wanting more.

His fingers began working at the buttons of her sweater, letting it fall open, exposing her, giving him access to continue his kitten-like petting of her stomach and sides. He began tracing the edges of her bra, dipping his fingers under the edges to stroke and tease her nipples to even harder diamond points.

Sitting up, he unbuttoned his own shirt as she watched. His nipples were hard too, set upon the platform of his strong chest. She reached up, running her hands up his stomach and over his chest, teasing his nipples right back. She slid her hands down, exploring the top edge of his jeans with her fingertips, enjoying the groan she heard from the back of his throat as she neared his trapped erection.

He reached for her jeans, unbuttoning the snap and zipper, then easing them down her legs and tossing them aside. Instead of reaching for the clasp, he scooped each breast out of the top of her bra, the lingerie supporting them into a deliciously rounded display.

Leaning down, he slowly licked around each areola, avoiding the nipples themselves, while his hands caressed the creamy mounds and his wife writhed in need beneath him.

"Please, Bill," she gasped.

He shook his head as he lowered it, running his kisses down her stomach, his hands stroking the lengths of her thighs all the way to her ankles, then back up to the edges of her soaking wet panties.

"Mmm. Mmm." He murmured against her aching pussy through the fabric, using his voice's vibration to stimulate her as his hands reached up and finally pinched her nipples.

"Ohh, Bill," she moaned, desperately raising her hips, her chest, her anything, to try and receive more under his teasing touches.

He slid up her body, his firm, muscular chest rubbing against her mound, her stomach, her needy nipples. Looking into her eyes, he said, "I'm going to taste you tonight. I'm going to taste you like the delicious little Candy you are. And you, my dear, are going to relax and enjoy it. We are in no rush."

His assertive dominance thrilled her and was extra heady when combined with his reassurance; he understood her preoccupation that it always took her "too long" to orgasm.

"We are in no rush at all," he repeated, "and I'm going to make you come and come and come."

Candace felt a strange mix of relaxing into the situation and an electric jolt of excitement, both at the same time.

His lips began working their way down her neck, nibbling now, nibbling lower, along her collarbone, onto her breasts. His hand slid gently, then gradually more firmly over her soaking panties, teasing the edges, lifting the fabric and brushing his fingertips over her slick lips.

She twisted and moaned beneath him, running her hands desperately over his shoulders and back, clutching at his firm ass, still encased in his jeans. Arching toward him, she lifted her chest, ground herself against his hand, her need becoming almost too much to be enjoyable.

Sensing this, he firmly sucked one nipple into his mouth, pulling it between his lips, circling it inside his mouth with his tongue. A relieved gasp came from her lips, leading him to do the same to her other nipple, while his fingers finally…finally! plunged inside her dripping pussy.

He began to pick up the pace, expertly sucking from one nipple to the other while he fucked her with two fingers, dragging his dripping digits up and over her clit, then sliding back down and inside her firmly.

Lost in sensation, Candace moaned and rode his hand, torn between wanting him to stay on her clit and loving the feel of him stretching her wide with his thick fingers. Her nails dug into his shoulder blades as he continued to lathe her nipples, her orgasm building already, sitting just beyond reach, needing just a little more.

Bill murmured into her ear, "Hmm, you like that baby? I thought you would." He withdrew his hand and rose up onto his knees. "But I'm not letting you come just yet." He began unbuttoning his jeans, lowering his zipper, her attention rapt on the impending view of his hard cock.

He stood and she gazed up at him as he removed his jeans and underwear, his hard-on so firm that it pointed straight up at his bellybutton.

"Mmm." Candace licked her lips, noticing a drop of pre-cum that dripped from the tip, making her feel desired, pleased that she could excite him that much.

Bill grasped his thickness in his hand, stroking it slowly, pumping it the way he knew she loved to watch. "Look what you do to me, Candace."

He was still standing up, while she was lying on the blanket. Rising to a kneeling position, she reached for him, wrapping her hand around his girth and leaning her mouth toward his glistening head.

"You want to suck it?" Bill teased. "I know you love to suck it. But only a little…I'm not letting you make me come yet."

She slid her lips over the head, down the shaft, and slowly pushed it to the very back of her throat as far as she could take it, then pulled back, sliding her lips up along its length and circling the tip with her tongue.

She knew just how he loved it; she had cultivated the perfect rhythm over the years. She also knew that the man in him had no such antsiness about the sameness of their sex life: a great blow job was a great blow job. Although now that she thought of it, over the years he had become more tame, less demanding. Less dominant and more respectful during their lovemaking.

41

Fuck respect, she thought. *I want to do him like he's never been done before.*

Clutching at his ass, she took him firmly down her throat, then pushed him back, creating a rhythm where he was fucking her mouth.

She could feel his hesitation; knew he would never want to hurt her. She could also feel the moment he decided to let go, to take all that she was willing to give.

He buried his hands in her hair on either side of her head and started controlling the rhythm himself, pushing himself deeply into her throat, then drawing all the way back to the tip. His pace quickened and she could feel him thickening, taste the drops of cum that were threatening to explode. She loved the sensation of making him so excited, of being both his loving wife and his hot little cock-sucking minx. She would have loved for him to bury himself to the hilt and come deeply into her throat, but he stopped, withdrawing from her mouth and saying, "Lie back down."

With a combination of excitement and disappointment, she did as he said, and he knelt down to slide her panties off and remove her bra. Completely naked under his gaze, she watched as he lowered himself to her thighs while maintaining eye contact with her and saying, "Remember, we're not hurrying."

He started licking the outer lips of her pussy, running his tongue up one side, across her clitoris, and down the other. He moaned against her, again using the vibration of his voice against her now-bare femininity. He kissed and sucked, drawing each lip into his mouth, then circling her pulsing clit with his flattened tongue.

At a leisurely pace, he reached up with both hands, pinching her nipples in the same rhythm as his tongue was circling. Candace spread her legs wider, trying to further expose her clit to him as he buried his face into her and lathed the sensitive button.

She began bucking against him, all restraint eliminated, with no thought of anything other than the pleasure that was building between her legs. Recognizing that she was so close, he brought his hands down and started fucking her dripping hole

42

with two fingers while keeping her lips spread wide with his other hand, exposing her clit like a jewel on a velvet display.

Lapping and circling with his tongue, fucking her with his fingers, pleasure surged through him as her orgasm washed over her in waves and he felt the pulsing, spasming feel of her contracting against his tongue and fingers.

He held still, keeping his mouth against her clit for another moment, not moving, knowing it would be too sensitive, but wanting to enjoy the feel of his woman being satisfied so thoroughly.

Before she fully finished contracting, he rose to his knees and slid his throbbing cock inside her.

"Oh God, oh Bill, I love it when you fuck me while I come!" She moaned and bucked beneath him as he rode her in the rhythm he knew she loved best, building her orgasm into a second crest of clamping down that he knew would force him to also let go.

"I know, baby. I know what you love," he said, looking right into her eyes as he exploded inside her.

They both understood that his words had a deeper meaning. And they both understood that at that moment, their marriage had clicked into another level of closeness that only the years of time and their willingness to be completely open had provided.

Artistic License

Kelly Lawrence

Joanna had seen plenty of high quality erotic art in her time. As managing director of The Red Room, a gallery specializing in erotic, sensual pieces of fine art and sculpture, she had the pleasure of feasting her eyes on a daily basis.

But this was something else. The newly-hung painting, called simply *Adam*, part of tomorrow's exhibition, had been invading Joanna's fantasies for the past two days. Even now she kept finding reasons to leave her office and walk across the gallery to sneak another glance.

It was a fairly straightforward nude in the classical style, beautifully done certainly, but it was the model that had caught Joanna's eye. Rather than a voluptuous young woman draped over a couch, it was a guy. A young, buff, totally sexy guy with his head hung back, eyes closed, and lips slightly parted, his lush lower lip begging to be kissed. A swathe of red fabric was draped over his legs and hips, but fell away to reveal an impressive cock, lying fat and soft against his muscled thigh. The artist had put so much detail into the painting it could almost be a photograph, and Joanna could easily imagine reaching out to touch him, watching him grow even bigger in her hands...or perhaps it was just too long since she'd gotten laid.

After an amicable divorce eighteen months ago, her love life had definitely been lacking. There was no shortage of offers, but Joanna hadn't met anyone who really stirred her passions and in any case, she found dating tedious. All that talking and dining and asking polite questions when what it really boiled down to was; did you want to have sex with each other? So far Joanna's answer had been *no*. Her thoughts wandered again to the painting in the gallery. Now there was a man she could definitely say *yes* to.

She said "Yes!" later that night, lying in a bed that was too big for one person, her hand working between her legs as she imagined the man from the painting with his mouth on her, imagined running her expensively manicured nails across his toned chest. Her "yes" came out as a long, drawn out moan as she climaxed. She rolled over in bed, physically satisfied at least, but felt a pang as she realized that the painting would no doubt be sold the next day, and *Adam* would be hanging on someone else's wall.

She woke the next morning, head still full of erotic images of *Adam*, and realized there may in fact be a way to assuage her fantasies. Hand trembling slightly, she flipped through her phone, looking for the contact she needed.

Later that day Joanna stood next to a prominent city politician and his wife, sipping her champagne and looking demure as they showered her with compliments. Inside, however, she was fizzing. The exhibition was a storming success and the buzz in the room was tangible. The one that had everyone talking was, of course, *Adam*. Although thrilled that it was a hit, Joanna found herself feeling almost possessive over the painting, part of her wanting to cover that perfect male form, shielding it from any eyes other than her own.

Hearing an excited murmur behind her, Joanna turned to see a young man entering the gallery looking nervous, and her stomach did a backflip.

It was him.

He caught her eye and she waved him over, her lips curving into a smile. It had been easy enough to get his contact details from the artist and to phone with an invitation to the exhibition. She had been surprised to discover that his name really was Adam; Joanna had assumed it was a reference to the primordial man, rather than the actual name of the model. In fact, before she heard his real and unmistakably male voice over the phone, she had never thought of him as being a real person at all: he had only come alive in her fantasies. Remembering the shuddering climax she had brought herself to last night over his image, Joanna felt a hot blush creep into her face as he approached.

As he grew closer she felt the slow burn of desire start between her thighs. He was as delicious as his painting; indeed the artist had captured the essence of him so perfectly that he could have just strolled out of the frame. Clad in jeans and a simple white shirt, his physique looked every bit as perfect as had been depicted. As for his face, the painting prepared her for his strong jawline and full mouth with that bee-stung lower lip that was begging to be bitten, but it hadn't revealed the intensity of those green eyes. She would have thought it impossible, but he was even more desirable, even more blatantly fuckable than his picture.

He appraised her with his eyes as he approached, giving her a knowing smile that made her cheeks burn. Although their conversation had been brief, Joanna hoped she had injected just enough desire into her voice for him to guess at her motives. Champagne flute in hand, she sauntered over to him, letting her hips sway under her tight skirt. He was gazing at her, watching her move toward him. It turned her on to have the object of her desire these past three days looking back at her with lust in his eyes, enough that she felt her nipples harden beneath the thin red silk of her blouse.

He took the hand she offered and lifted it to his lips, his eyes never leaving hers. Joanna felt a frisson of pleasure run through her as his mouth grazed her skin. She wanted him, she decided, and soon.

"You've attracted quite a crowd," she murmured, as the small gathering standing admiring *Adam* started to approach them, no doubt to admire the real thing.

"To be honest," he lowered his voice so that she had to lean into him slightly, catching his clean, masculine smell, "I didn't think there would be so many people here. I was hoping we could be a bit more...private."

Hardly believing her own daring, Joanna slipped her arm through his.

"Why don't we get some refreshments?" she said lightly, her stomach churning. She couldn't remember ever being so physically affected by a man. She looked down at her arm linked

46

through his, at her scarlet nails against his thick, tanned forearms, and wanted to run them up and down his skin. Or preferably his back. To grip those firm ass cheeks as he plunged in and out of her. A slow burn began in her lower belly as the images filled her mind, and judging by the path his eyes were taking along the curves of her body, he was seeing something similar. He made no protest as she steered him into her office, and Joanna smiled at the sudden sense of power she felt when she closed the door and turned to him, letting her desire blaze in her eyes.

He took a step toward her, his tongue flickering over his lips as if nervous, and Joanna closed the gap between them and wound her arms around his neck, her eyes fixed on that lush mouth. She saw his throat move as he swallowed, felt the tremble in his strong hands as they slid around her, cupping her ass, and she smiled with the knowledge that right now, he was hers for the taking.

Their lips touched, tentatively at first, then he crushed her to him and ground his mouth against hers so that she could feel the scrape of his stubble against her skin. His tongue plunged her mouth in a way that made her think instantly of other parts of him entering her, and an involuntary moan escaped her. He was, as the painting had promised, all raw male. She pushed her hips against his and felt him hard through his jeans, straining for release. Determined to remain in control she stepped back and took a deep breath, letting her eyes roam over him slowly.

"Strip," she said softly, relishing the look of surprise in his eyes, and allowing herself a flicker of triumph as he pulled his shirt over his head.

He was as perfectly formed as his painting, all chiseled lines and smooth hardness, and she raked her nails lightly across his chest as he unzipped his jeans. They fell to the floor, followed quickly by his underwear, and his cock sprang eagerly into her hand. She gripped him firmly, feeling her pussy twitch in response as he groaned, and she pushed him back toward her desk.

"I want you inside me," she said, seeing his eyes grow dark with desire as she hitched up her skirt with her free hand. Perched on her desk, he reached for her, pulling her panties urgently to the side and testing her with his fingertips to find her already swollen, already wet.

She straddled him, kissing him roughly as his hands went inside her blouse to knead her breasts, using her own hand to guide him inside her. She gasped at the thickness of him, at the feel of him straining against her opening, and steadying herself against his chest, Joanna buried her face against his neck and began to move in a sensuous rhythm, rocking her hips against his. She needed this; allowing herself this moment of total abandon, and she bit his neck to keep from moaning as he kneaded her ass cheeks, grinding her onto him. She picked up her pace, riding him until she could feel the tension building within her, feel the waves about to break over her body, and she tipped her head back and rocked urgently as she felt her climax approaching.

Adam gripped her hips, the sight of this beautiful woman fucking him, lost in her own pleasure, driving him toward his own release. She bit her lip as she clenched around him, her orgasm so intense she felt her toes curl, and he came seconds later, letting his breath out in a low growl.

They shuddered against each other, slick with each other's juices, then she stepped back, tugging her skirt down even as he reached for her.

"I have to get back to the exhibition," she said softly, leaning in and kissing him swiftly on the lips.

Joanna left him tugging his clothes back on, blowing him a kiss over her shoulder as she sauntered off. All Adam could do was gaze after her, watching her swaying figure walk away from him with the languorous moves of a thoroughly satisfied woman.

The Sensual Garden

J.R. Read

Ruth heard the sound of David's cowboy boots crunch onto her gravel pathway. Her gardener approached wearing his trademark Stetson and sexy smile.

"Good morning, Ruth. Gorgeous bikini, by the way. Love the color on you. Where do you want me?"

David seemed unfazed that his employer was lying on a sun lounger, wearing little more than four triangles of fabric.

Ruth returned his smile and replied, "Good morning, David. I figured you would do your usual tidy up please. I'll be around today. I'm going to sunbathe and take advantage of this weather. I won't be in your way, will I?"

"Sunbathe away, Ruth. Just promise me you won't go topless and distract me. I don't think my aging heart could take it!"

Ruth replied with a laugh, "David you're thirty-four, that's hardly old. Wait until you hit forty-five, and then you'll know what old is."

Ruth was forty-six but felt in her twenties when she was around this man. She'd been married for too long to a man who'd forgotten she existed. Her two children had long since flown the nest and although Ruth had her career in teaching, she always felt there was something important missing in her life. Her sex life had ceased some time ago and she had to admit, she did miss the intimacy.

A sensual woman who was very in tune with her emotions, she took pleasure in many things, one of those being her garden. She had spent time creating a space very personal to

49

her, but since her promotion the previous winter, Ruth had less time to spend on the upkeep of her garden. Then one day she stumbled upon on an advertisement that caught her eye: "Do you want a man on his hands and knees, at your beck and call? If yes, then I'm your man! No gardening job too big or too small. Call David, I can service your every need."

Ruth loved the flirty, direct style. She also thought it was quite a creative way to advertise. She called the number and David appeared at her door the next day.

The minute she opened the door, Ruth was attracted to him. He wore jeans, a shirt with his sleeves rolled up (*not afraid of hard work,* she thought), cowboy boots (this made her smile), and a Stetson (which made her smile even more). He had the bluest eyes and the sexiest smile she had seen in a long time. He also had a hint of stubble on his jaw, and Ruth loved that look on a man.

David extended his hand and Ruth took it, enjoying the feel of his rough, work-hardened skin.

"Hi, I'm David, you must be Ruth. My horse is tethered up at the gate. Is that okay?" he said, with a mischievous twinkle in those gorgeous eyes.

Before she could answer, he added, "Only joking, your face is a picture! I am a cowboy in waiting though. Feel like I've missed my calling."

Ruth instantly liked David. She wanted to get to know him; he had just secured himself a regular gardening job.

They spent the next hour walking around her garden, with David making notes and complimenting her on her planting schemes and overall design. Then he asked, "What inspired you to create this particular garden, Ruth? It really is beautiful."

"I wanted a space that would stimulate all my senses."

"Do you get all the pleasure you need, Ruth? Does it do it for you?" he asked seriously.

She wondered if he was still talking about the garden. "Yes David, my garden gives me the stimuli I hoped it would," she said carefully.

They agreed that he would spend three hours each week maintaining the grounds, and she asked how long he had been in the gardening business.

50

"Well, I love gardening. I always have ever since I was a child. When I was seven, I asked Santa for a bag of compost. He obliged and the rest is history. I've run my own landscaping company for nine years. I love making dreams come true, pure and simple." David smiled and stretched. His shirt came loose from his jeans and afforded her a glimpse of his torso. It was taut and tanned, and she caught sight of what she liked to think of as his "Happy Trail."

She suddenly became hot and had to look away. David stayed in that position for longer than was necessary, apparently aware of the effect he was having on her—and he seemed to be enjoying it.

Ruth blushed and said, "I won't keep you any longer David, I'm sure you're a very busy man. Unless there's anything else you need from me?"

David held Ruth's gaze for what seemed an eternity. "No," he said slowly, "I think you've given me everything I want for now."

With his words ringing in her ears, he winked at her and walked away, leaving Ruth with the sight of his perfect jean-clad butt, strutting back down her path. *What a flirt!* Ruth thought, *I'll bet he has a whole string of horny, lonely female clients fawning all over him.*

That was back in March. It was now June and David had tended her grounds each week since then. With Ruth teaching in school, they had very little contact. Usually, Ruth was coming in from work as David was packing away. He always took time to talk to her and he always complimented her. Today was the first time she had been home for any extended period of time while David was around.

It was a cloudless summer's day, and Ruth intended to take full advantage of the weather and her garden. She had positioned her lounge chair in her favorite part of the garden and settled herself with a good book. She wore a halter-neck bikini that had ties at either side of her hips. Knowing that David might be around, she had chosen one that she felt flattered her figure, which was curvy and still good. Ruth looked after herself and took pride in her appearance, even though she had no one to appreciate it. She still wore her brunette hair long and was rarely without makeup. Today she wore her hair loose and opted for a natural look of mascara and a nude lip gloss.

David had gotten Ruth hot and bothered, complimenting her bikini and joking about her going topless. *I wonder if he'll go topless. I would love to see his chest!* Ruth longed for just a little peek, as her imagination had been working overtime since she'd met him.

Before she knew it she had voiced her thoughts! David threw his head back and laughed, "I have standards to keep, Ms. James. I have too much respect for my clients. I always keep my shirt on. Hope you're not too disappointed." He smirked. "Even my hat stays put. I would need to be extremely hot and sticky to remove either."

With that, David turned and left Ruth feeling a little foolish. She pulled her sunglasses over her eyes and lay back down to hide her embarrassment.

Relaxing, she thought of the joy her garden brought her. As she had told David all those months previously, her goal had been to create a place that stimulated all of her senses. She had achieved that, she felt. Her thoughts drifted to how each sense was aroused.

Her rose garden provided her with the beautiful aroma of Deep Secret. This rose was selected for its rich, sensual, deep red color and full blooms. Ruth thought this to be an incredibly sexy flower.

Her hearing and touch were evoked by her beloved pampas grass. She loved the way the grass moved in the breeze, the delicate sound it made. Ruth also loved the way the grass felt. She would often trail her hands over the full heads and marvel at the soft fronds of grass, in such contrast to their firm, woody stalks.

To Ruth, the taste of summer was definitely strawberries. She had several bushes that yielded copious amounts of the delicious fruit.

As she baked in the sun, she was unaware that her gardener was standing several yards away, watching her. Although she was aware of his innocent flirting, she was also oblivious to the fact that David was really attracted to Ruth

James. He loved older women, the confidence they exuded, their hang-ups over their bodies long since gone.

Ruth ticked all of David's boxes: she was a blue-eyed brunette, curvy, had a great personality, and she was also totally unaware of the effect she had on him. He'd wanted her since the day he'd met her. He was constantly being propositioned by the women he worked for, but he had a rule that he never touched them.

David knew that he was about to break his self-imposed rule. He wanted to show this gorgeous woman just how much pleasure her garden could evoke. He watched as she sunbathed, her fingers idly tracing down her tummy. David instantly knew what he was going to do, and off he went to collect some props.

When he returned, Ruth was in the same position. He stood at the end of her sun lounger with a basket of wares from the garden. She sensed David's presence and opened her eyes. She didn't dare speak, as she could see the unmistakable lust in his eyes as they traveled the length of her body.

Rather than feel self-conscious, she felt empowered. She pushed her glasses onto her head and looked intently at him. He walked toward her, placed the basket on the ground, and leaned in close to her ear.

In a low, husky voice, he said, "I'm going to show you just how much pleasure you can get from your garden."

As he spoke, Ruth felt his breath on her ear, his stubble brushing lightly against her cheek, and she could smell the leather of his Stetson along with a subtle, musky mixture of cologne and sweat.

"Close your eyes, Ruth, and relax."

She did exactly as she was told. As she lay in anticipation, she became aware of something being placed in her hair at the side of her head. She smelled the unmistakable scent of her Deep Secret rose. *How does he know it's my favorite?*

She felt something soft on her cheek, moving to trace her lips, her neck. *What is it?* Whatever it was, it felt delicious, especially as it traveled onto her chest. Ruth held her breath, waiting for her breasts to be touched, but no, the featherlike object bypassed them and moved to her tummy.

Her bellybutton was traced and then the outline of her bikini bottom. Ruth opened one eye and almost laughed as she saw that it was a length of pampas grass being used as an erotic tickling stick. The panicle of the grass was now near her pussy, and she was desperate to know how it would feel. David deprived her of that feeling though, as he moved the grass down the insides of her thighs. He traced the length of her legs and began to move back up her body.

"Did you ever realize that pampas grass has such properties, Ruth? Did you know it was so erotic? How does it make you feel?" His voice was deep and smooth.

"I want more David, please give me more," she nearly moaned.

"What about if I touched you here?"

Ruth gasped as he ran the head of the grass over her right bikini-clad breast, causing her nipple to harden instantly. She gripped the sides of the sun lounger as the same happened to her left breast.

"Goodness Ruth, I've hardly touched them. What will you be like when my tongue flicks over those nipples?"

Fuck, this is really happening! was all she could think.

Ruth felt a change of texture on her skin, at the top of her breast; something hooked under the fabric of one of the triangles. She realized it was the woody stalk of the grass and it was being used to push the fabric away, to expose her. The sequence repeated on the opposite side. Ruth was effectively topless, lying there desperate for more.

David brought the soft grass back to her breasts and swept the soft head across, from one to the other. Ruth gently rocked and arched her back to gain as much stimulation as possible.

"You have beautiful breasts, Ruth. I have dreamed of touching them for a long time."

With that, David bent and lightly licked around each nipple in turn. Ruth moaned with pleasure, her sounds spurring him on as he took one breast in his hand and gently kneaded the flesh while he expertly sucked on the other nipple.

Ruth's hands came up to David's head, which was still, remarkably, clad in his Stetson!

"Can I please take this off?" she asked.

"Do you think it's hot enough for me to remove it?" David replied with his mouth still working on her nipple.

"Fuck, yes. It's hot David, please." He stood and Ruth noticed just how hot things had gotten. David's jeans bulged with an unmistakable erection.

"See what you do to me, woman," he said.

Ruth felt like a sex goddess, having that effect on such an attractive, sexy man. He knocked his hat to the floor, revealing dark, closely-cut hair. She held her breath as he loosened his t-shirt and lifted it above his head, watching as he revealed his muscled chest with a fair covering of the same dark hairs.

"You've distracted me, woman. Where was I? Your breasts have had some attention, but I feel there are other parts I'm neglecting. I want you to keep your eyes open now Ruth, I want you to watch the next part."

Ruth's pussy twitched in anticipation.

David picked up the pampas grass. Ruth looked down her body, her breasts now free of the fabric, which was bunched up on either side of them.

David was loosening one of the ties at her hip. As he opened it, he used the stem to move the flimsy fabric aside, exposing her mound. This time it was David's turn to catch his breath.

His eyes narrowed and glazed over. "What an amazing little cunt," he said in a low voice. He licked his lips and, excruciatingly slowly, he moved the head of the grass to the top of Ruth's pubic mound and began to pull its soft top along her crack.

She bit her lower lip and raised her pelvis up to meet the head as the feathers traced her labia and moved down toward her anus. She moaned in delight, desperate to feel it on her clit. She needed the pressure increased and sought the relief of an orgasm.

David read her thoughts. "Easy baby," he said, "I know what you want."

"Then do it David. Please, give me what I want."

"What do you want Ruth? Tell me."

"My clit," she gasped. "Rub it on my clit."

"Oh, like this?" He slid the grass into her cleft and found the spot. "There?" he asked, a teasing confidence in his voice.

"Yes," she breathed, "right there!"

David rolled the piece of grass around as Ruth ground against it, her breasts moving as her rhythm increased. She sought more pressure than the delicate grass could give.

David suddenly stopped what he was doing.

"Please, don't stop," she said desperately.

"Don't worry baby, I'm certainly not stopping. What's the taste of summer, Ruth?"

Her mind raced. "Strawberries," she answered.

"I promise you, Ruth, you will never have tasted strawberries quite as delicious as these."

David pulled Ruth down the lounger and told her to draw her knees up. He knelt at the foot and held up a swollen, ripened red berry.

Thoughts whirled through Ruth's head. What was he going to do with it? Was he going to use it to stimulate her?

As though reading her mind, he lowered the berry down to her quim, using his free hand to part her labia. Ruth felt an electric current race through her core as his fingers touched her. He held her open as he rubbed the tip of the strawberry over her hole, before pushing gently and inserting it inside her. Ruth cried out. As he pulled it out, he moved it up and over her aching clit, spreading her love juices. He repeated the sequence several more times, each time bringing her closer to coming.

Her breathing became ragged and she was desperate for the release her body needed. David once again plunged the berry deep inside her dripping wet pussy. This time he turned it, and she could feel the tips of his fingers at her entrance. He slowly pulled the strawberry out and brought it to his mouth. Ruth watched in disbelief as he licked the sides. She had never seen anything as sensual in her entire life.

His eyes held hers as he took a bite, the juices—a mixture of the ripe berry and her own—dripping down his lips. "Do you want to taste?" he asked.

Ruth nodded, as she was incapable of speaking. He lowered his head to hers and told her to lick his mouth. She did so greedily. Like a lioness feeding, she licked and sucked at his mouth. It tasted fantastic, the delicious fruit and her pussy juices mixed with David's saliva.

56

"I told you it would taste good. Each time you eat strawberries now, you will remember this," he whispered against her mouth. "But we're not finished yet."

He closed his mouth over hers, his tongue searching hers out. He fisted his hands into her hair, catching the stem of the rose as he did so. As his mouth possessed her, Ruth flicked her tongue against his and took his lower lip between her teeth, gently biting him.

David let out a low growl. "You have been driving me crazy, Ruth. You have no idea how fucking sexy you are. I could fuck you senseless, right now. But I would come too soon, that's how much you turn me on."

He broke free of the kiss and once again Ruth caught sight of his arousal. She reached for his groin but he caught her hand.

"Not yet," he scolded her. "I want to make you come first."

He handed Ruth a fresh berry and said, "I want to watch as you use this to pleasure yourself."

Ruth was shocked, but took the fruit. David once again took his position, on his knees at the foot of the sunbed. Ruth laughed and reminded David of his advertisement, promising a man on his knees.

"Ruth, for you, I would be permanently on my knees."

"I'll bet you say that to all your ladies," she said lightheartedly.

David stopped and looked at her seriously, "I want you to know that I don't make a habit of this, Ruth. You're a very special woman. You do believe me, don't you?" She laughed out of embarrassment. "Please, Ruth," David searched her face, his eyes begging to be believed. In that moment, she knew he was telling the truth.

"I believe you, David," she said sincerely. She did believe him, but now was not the time for a lengthy heart-to-heart. "Now, where were we? Oh yes," she said, as she licked the berry and placed it against her vulva.

David swallowed and watched intently as she tantalized him by moving the fruit agonizingly slowly up and down her glistening slit.

Ruth felt like an exhibitionist. She had never done anything like this before, although she felt that she'd had, at one time, a fulfilling sex life.

Obviously, she had never lived! Who would have thought she would be lying here, outdoors, playing with her pussy while a hunky gardener watched. This was a real-life porn movie and she was the female star!

Ruth brought the fruit to her mouth and held eye contact with David as she sucked the liquid from the tip. David moved his right hand down to the crotch of his jeans and rubbed his erection. This action sent Ruth wild and spurred her on. She quickly placed the berry back on her clit and circled it around the swollen button, while with her free hand, she reached down and inserted two fingers into her pussy.

She was very wet, and she wasn't sure whether it was from the strawberry or it was her own body making the moisture. Ruth was so close to coming that she could feel the familiar tingles building inside her.

David sensed this and he grabbed the berry from her, saying, "You're one sexy woman Ruth. I've got to taste that gorgeous-looking cunt."

Ruth removed her fingers and offered them to David who hungrily accepted them, sucking and licking her love potion. She took hold of either side of his head and pushed his face into her waiting pussy, thrusting her hips up as he buried his face into her.

David's tongue lapped away on her throbbing clit. He stiffened the tip and flicked all around before placing his mouth over the entire swelling, and sucked.

Ruth almost screamed—she had never experienced anything quite like it. Her back arched and her grip tightened on David's head, holding him firmly in place as she frantically rubbed against him. His bristly stubble accentuated the arousal as Ruth reached the point of no return.

She cried out, "Fuck, David, you're making me come," as she exploded against his mouth. Waves of pleasure washed over her and she writhed with them as David held her legs in place and continued to lick and kiss and suck.

He didn't allow her to come down. When she became overly sensitive after her orgasm, David worked through it and

58

relentlessly kept at it. Because her clit was so sensitized, she was now experiencing brand new sensations.

In Ruth's experience, once a man had made a woman come, that was his signal to fuck her and allow himself to orgasm. David was obviously a new breed of man. A breed that Ruth liked, very much.

He lifted his eyes and looked directly at her, keeping visual contact as he reached for her right hand. He replaced his mouth for her fingers and he moved them using his own hand.

Ruth felt herself, soaking wet. She felt the folds of velvety skin, her swollen clit. David moved her fingers along the entire length of her. He sent her fingers right down to the puckered skin of her butt hole, smearing the juices everywhere. He brought them back up and held them over her love button. He instructed her to rub as he licked in between her fingers.

It was so incredibly erotic and intimate, it sent her over the edge. This had never happened to Ruth, another orgasm so soon after the first.

"Oh, David yes!" She cried out, as she came for what felt like an eternity. Her body felt like it had shattered into a million pieces. She was completely sated, but could not get enough of this man. She felt like a nymphomaniac, wanting this to go on forever.

Finally, her body relaxed onto the sunbed, and she could feel her love juices running down between her buttocks and soaking the cushion beneath her.

"Did you enjoy that, Ruth?" he asked.

"What do you think?" she replied breathlessly.

"Now it's your turn," she said, as she shifted position and sat up to reach for his zipper. She moved to the edge of the lounge chair, her bikini bottoms hanging on by one tie, her breasts hanging heavy and free.

As she unzipped him, David reached down and rubbed her nipple between his finger and thumb.

"Your tits are fantastic, Ruth. You are all woman."

Ruth smiled. She certainly felt like a woman, for the first time in years. A sex-mad, insatiable woman at that! She was fast embracing this new Ruth, as she undid the belt and button at his waistband.

She felt a jolt of excitement as she lowered the band of David's boxers and freed his stiff cock, then gasped at the sight of it. It was thick and meaty and ready for action. She held it in one hand and eased his boxers further down to release his balls. She traced her long nails under them and up, from the root to the tip of his rigid manhood.

David let out a low moan and she looked up at him. What a sight! He stood looking down at her, his body glistening with a sheen of perspiration. His abs were flexed and his jaw was clenched.

"Suck my cock, Ruth."

She didn't need asking twice. She used her tongue to trace the outline and then licked down the shaft, around his balls, her hands slowly pumping him. When he thrust toward her she responded by pulling his foreskin back and flicking her tongue around the helmet.

David gripped her hair and moaned. She continued to play with him before she deep throated him; she could barely accommodate his length. She slid her mouth back up and sucked, following with her hands as she kept the rhythm going.

Suddenly David said, "Please stop. Ruth. You're going to make me come."

"And the problem is?" Ruth answered seductively.

"The problem is, woman, is that I need to feel that cunt around my cock, and I want to fuck you."

"The problem is," Ruth countered, "is that I want to taste you. I want to taste your cum and feel it shooting down my throat."

"You sexy fucking bitch," David growled as he tore at the final tie of her bikini. It offered little resistance and fell to the ground.

He practically threw her onto her knees and bent her over the lounger. He was behind her in seconds, using one knee to push her legs apart. The fingers of both hands were at her pussy; he opened her up and she felt the tip of his cock, slick with pre-cum, nudging at her entrance.

"Do you know how much I have fantasized about this Ruth? About how good it would feel to take you, to feel your hot

60

little cunt swallowing my cock?" At that moment, he thrust fully into her and she pushed back into him.

She moaned loudly as he filled her totally. Ruth could feel the metal of his belt buckle slamming against her butt and the rough denim of his jeans rubbing against her naked thighs. She felt her pelvic muscles contract against his shaft.

"Fuck, that's better than I could ever have imagined," David said between clenched teeth.

He slid his cock all the way out before ramming it back in, right up to the hilt. He took a firm grip of her hips and repeatedly thrust into her, building them both into a frenzied pace.

Suddenly, he slowed the rhythm and reached around with his hand to find her clit. With one hand he rubbed, and with the other he found her left breast, mirroring the action with her nipple.

This can't be happening, Ruth thought. She knew the signs, and without a doubt, she was going to come again. She opened her legs wider and pushed back against him. He responded by thrusting into her.

The feeling of his cock filling her and his fingers on her clit and nipple pushed her to the brink, "Don't stop, please, David. Make me come again, please!"

He increased the speed and the pressure, and once again Ruth cried out as her orgasm took hold of her. She stiffened and clenched, as the waves of pleasure washed over and over her.

She had barely stopped contracting when David ground his hips into her. She could feel his balls stroking against her mound and she reached between her legs and pressed them into her as she writhed against them.

"Oh fuck!" David cried, "you're so damn sexy, woman!"

As he thrust fast and hard into her, Ruth held tightly to the lounge chair and took it, loving the power she had, to turn this man on so much.

David withdrew his cock, pulled her head up, and said, "You wanted to taste this. Well come on then."

Ruth took him deep into her mouth and her hands slid up and down the shaft as David thrust into her.

"Don't stop Ruth, I'm coming!" David growled like an animal as he held her head in place by her hair.

She could smell the pungent aroma of her rose as he came hard in her mouth. His seed spilled down her throat and escaped out of the sides of her lips.

She looked up and saw that David's eyes were completely glazed over and his teeth were gritted. He thrust one last time as the last drops of his man cream shot into her mouth.

She swallowed and then slowly released his cock, licking it clean, not missing a drop. She used the tip of his slowly receding erection to push the escaped droplets back into her mouth.

"Wow!" David said, truly sounding amazed.

"Wow yourself," she replied.

"Well, Ms. James, has your garden stimulated *all* of your senses?" he asked, once again with his mischievous twinkle.

"Not really sure," Ruth replied cheekily. "I think there are still some heights I haven't reached. Maybe next week we could try the bamboo and the rhubarb!"

Extra Money

Michael Bracken

I took extra time preparing for the evening, wanting to look sexy without crossing the line into slutty. I finally chose a simple black cocktail dress that reached mid-thigh, that hinted at but did not actually reveal cleavage, and that hugged my curves like a fine Italian sports car on a mountain road. Beneath it I wore black bikini panties and a black push-up bra. I accented my apparel with pearl stud earrings and a single strand of pearls, and then stepped into my crimson, spike-heeled pumps that matched the polish on both my fingernails and my toenails. After a last glance in the mirror to assure myself that my makeup was appropriate and that every strand of my shoulder-length auburn hair was in place, I phoned for a taxi.

Less than twenty minutes later the cab delivered me to Slingbacks, a drinking establishment so tony that a doorman held the cab door open for me, escorted me across the sidewalk to the entrance, and held that door as well.

After I stepped inside, I hesitated a moment to look around and let my eyes adjust to the dim light. The bar sat only six and none of the high-backed, black leather stools were occupied. Instead, Slingbacks' early evening patrons mostly sat in the dozen darkened booths that lined the left side and back walls. Only one middle-aged couple sat at any of the half-dozen tables in the center of the room, and they were engaged in a quiet conversation that had them leaning toward each other, enjoying one another's company. A similarly aged cocktail waitress, obviously hired for her ability and not her sex appeal, moved through the room with quiet efficiency.

I took a seat at the bar where I could see and be seen, and ordered a martini with a twist of lemon from a sharply dressed bartender old enough to be my grandfather. Slow and deliberate, he prepared my drink with nary a wasted motion and placed it before me.

After I took a sip, he asked, "Is it satisfactory?"

"Quite," I replied.

"Shall I run a tab?"

"Please."

"As you wish," he said. Then he faded to the other end of the bar, where he waited patiently for the waitress to bring him an order.

I nursed my drink and watched the room's reflection in the mirror behind the bar. The lighting was such that I couldn't see into the depths of the booths, and not much happened until I finished my drink. When I did, the waitress approached the bar and whispered to the bartender, and soon he slid a fresh drink in front of me. "It's from the gentleman at the end."

I turned and watched a pug-faced man with too many diamonds on his fingers lean out of the far booth and raise a glass in my direction. As I returned my attention to the bartender, I said, "Tell him thank you, but no thank you."

The bartender whispered my words to the waitress, who passed them along to my pug-faced benefactor. As he disappeared back into the darkness of his booth, I heard "Come here often?"

I'd been paying attention to the far end of the room so I hadn't been watching the mirror and hadn't seen anyone approach from my other side. I turned to see a handsome man near my age sitting on the other side of me. He wore a dark blue suit over a navy blue tie and pale blue button-down shirt. He was clean-shaven, and his dark hair held just a hint of silver at the temples.

I said, "My first time."

"Mine, too."

I uncrossed my legs and recrossed them in the other direction, letting one spike-heeled pump dangle from my toes.

My new companion caught the bartender's attention. "What she's having."

64

After the bartender stepped away to prepare his martini, he introduced himself as Paul and asked my name.

Deborah seemed too plain so I lied. "Tiffany."

Paul seemed amused. He captured my left hand in his hands and ran the tips of his fingers over the indentions on my ring finger where my wedding band had been until a few hours earlier. "Do you do this often?"

"Not often."

"And your husband?"

I wet my lips with the tip of my tongue. "He's away on business."

The bartender delivered Paul's martini and faded away. Paul reached for it, took a sip, and then twirled the glass with his fingers. Finally, he asked, "How much?"

I named a price.

He considered. Then he drained his martini and paid our bar tabs.

*****

We arrived at my house in no time, and I led Paul to the bedroom with only the moonlight filtering through the windows to guide us through the darkened house. As soon as I closed the bedroom door he pulled me into his arms and covered my mouth with his.

I hesitated at first, thinking a kiss was too intimate for the price I'd quoted, but I couldn't resist and I returned his kisses with my own. Soon our tongues met and our kisses were deeper, longer, and breath-stealing.

He unzipped my dress. When I shook the sleeves off my shoulders, the dress slithered down the curves of my body and pooled at my feet. I pushed Paul's jacket off his shoulders and it dropped to the floor with my dress. Then I unknotted and unthreaded his tie, unbuttoned his shirt and pulled it free of his slacks. When I unfastened his belt and unzipped his fly he stopped me. He sat on the end of the bed, untangled himself from his clothing, and quickly peeled everything off. Paul's erection rose majestically from the dark nest of hair at his crotch, so long and thick and rigid that I felt certain I was going to enjoy my annual moneymaking venture.

I stepped out of the clothing pooled at my feet and turned to face Paul. I stood before him wearing only my jewelry, bra, panties, and spiked heels. I reached behind my back, unfastened my bra, and let it drop away to reveal my breasts. He reached for them, cupped them in his hands, and stroked my rapidly stiffening nipples with the balls of his thumbs.

Then he hooked his thumbs in the waistband of my panties and pulled them down with one quick tug, revealing my denuded pubic mound. When my panties reached my knees, he released them. I stepped out of them and pushed him back. Then I climbed on the bed, straddled him, and knee-walked up his body until I straddled his face.

"Eat me," I commanded as I grabbed the headboard and lowered my bare pussy onto Paul's face. The curtains were open above the headboard and I could see the moonlit backyard. The swing set, the tricycles, and the lawn that had not been cut while my husband was away all reminded me of how inappropriate it was to bring a strange man to our bed, and those thoughts excited me even more.

Paul obliged my command. His tongue snaked out and he traced the long, slick slit of my female opening with its tip. A moment later, he reached between my thighs and pulled my swollen pussy lips apart. He sucked my loose inner lips between his teeth and nibbled on them, something only my husband had ever done, and I softly moaned with pleasure.

He reached up and cupped my breasts again. My turgid nipples strained against his palms. I covered his hands with mine and squeezed, showing him rather than telling him what I wanted.

As he massaged my breasts, Paul buried his tongue inside me and drove it in and out, painting my inner walls with his saliva. Then he found my swollen clit and spanked it with his tongue. My hips began to move as his oral caresses continued, and I gripped the headboard tightly to brace myself as I rode his face. I felt my orgasm building, felt my entire body begin to tense as my pussy clenched and unclenched with each stroke of Paul's tongue.

And then I came.

My entire body quivered, and I had to reach between my thighs to stop Paul's tongue.

66

As I sat on his face catching my breath, I realized Paul was paying me to please him, but I was receiving all the pleasure. That wasn't right.

I slid backward until I straddled his waist. I reached between my thighs, grabbed Paul's thick erection, and positioned the spongy-smooth head between my saliva-slickened pussy lips. Then I dropped my full weight upon him, forcing his erection deep inside me.

He grabbed my hips as I pushed myself up and dropped back down, and he moved with me and against me, thrusting his erection upward as I lowered myself around it.

I thought of the man beneath me. I thought of my husband. I thought of missing him and of having my needs unfulfilled while he was away. I thought of the nights I'd had to pleasure myself whenever we were apart during our first few years of marriage, and how I'd stumbled upon a profitable solution.

I'd been cleaning the bathroom that afternoon and had forgotten to return my wedding band to its rightful place on my finger before I left the house that evening. After leaving my daughters with my mother-in-law, I had gone to a bar near the train station. While there, an attractive man had approached me, flirted with me, purchased a drink for me, and had proposed a solution to my mounting frustration. I'd used my real name that night and had been surprised to find money on my nightstand when I woke alone the next morning.

I had not used my real name since.

While I thought of that first time, I also thought of my husband and how much he desired me upon his return home, about how hard he worked to please me in bed and out, about how his fantasy desires and my own could fit so nicely together. And as those thoughts ricocheted through my mind, I rode Paul hard and I rode him fast. My breasts and the strand of pearls around my neck slapped against my chest as the bedsprings groaned in protest. He seemed insatiable beneath me and I came first, my entire body tensing like a steel spring that suddenly released.

That didn't stop Paul. He drove up into me as my pussy clenched and unclenched around his thick shaft. Again and again and again, and then with a groan he erupted within me.

I collapsed on top of him, my breasts flattened against his muscular chest, and he wrapped one arm around me. With his other hand he pushed hair away from my face and stared into my eyes.

Fully satisfied, I whispered, "How long are you in town?"

"Just for the night," Paul whispered in return. "Tomorrow morning I return to my wife."

"She's a lucky woman."

"Not as lucky as your husband."

I rolled off of Paul and watched as he slid from the bed and dressed. He left two crisp one-hundred-dollar bills on the dresser and let himself out. After he was gone, I wrapped my arms around the pillow, inhaled the lingering scent of my lover, and drifted off to sleep.

*****

I woke to the sound of pans clattering in the kitchen. I slipped out of bed, pulled on a terrycloth robe, and cinched it tight. I retrieved my wedding band from the nightstand drawer and slipped it on before heading to the other end of the house.

My husband and our daughters, who had returned home from my mother-in-law's house while I was sleeping, were preparing breakfast and making quite a mess of things. I walked up behind my husband and wrapped my arms around him. In his ear I whispered, "The extra hundred was a nice touch."

Paul whispered back, "You were worth every bit of it."

Play Date

Katherine Crighton

My baby has just gone to sleep, so the house has got to stay quiet; the smallest creak will wake her. As for Brian, his littlest is only attending camp for the morning session, so we've got just an hour or so to have our fun and to do it as quietly as possible.

When I shut the door to the nursery and ease my way back down the hall, the front door is already closing. Brian, in running clothes, leans against it, then raises his eyebrows in a question and looks back the way I came. He's a natural dusky tan, with a runner's build and short dark hair streaked with a little bit of gray. We met about a year ago in a single parents' group. So far, I don't think any of the other parents have figured out that we've been having our own "play dates" for the last four months.

I listen for a moment, but I don't hear anything from the nursery. I flash a grin at Brian, and he reaches out for me and tugs me close. His body feels firm and warm through my yoga pants and v-neck. He's already half hard, too. He presses his hand against the small of my back, rocking his cock against me just a little, and he brushes my hair back from my ear.

"Hey, Anna," he whispers.

"Hey," I murmur back. His t-shirt outlines his chest, just enough that I can see the peak of his nipple through it. I run my hand over him, tease his nipple with my fingertips, and nibble at his jaw, making him gasp.

Discovering how sensitive he is was an accident the first time. Just a hug that had gone on too long, two friends who weren't sure if we were something more, and my hand drifted over his small, tight nipple as we broke apart, a little bit by

69

accident and a little bit on purpose...and he gasped and just looked at me with heat in his eyes.

It's definitely no accident when I do it again now, and this time there's no hesitation on his part when he reaches down and grabs me by the ass with both hands, lifts me, presses me close, and carries me to the living room. I laugh silently, twining my arms around his neck and my legs around his waist, letting each of his steps rock me against his trapped hard-on.

He drops me gracelessly onto the dark blue couch, ending half-sprawled on top of me. I don't mind; it means his face is right there, those eyes looking into mine just as hot and thoughtful as the day we first kissed. His lips cant up in a half-smile, and I can't help but lean up to kiss him, to taste his mouth, mostly familiar but still deliciously exotic.

His hands outline the curve of my hips, the curve of my belly, the rise and fall of my mound, and his fingers tease at the line of my pussy before he pulls down my pants entirely. We used to be more shy about this, more hesitant, but there's only so much time between when my baby goes to sleep and when Brian has to leave to pick up his little girl from camp. Sometimes we'll play at being new lovers, Brian kissing his way along the outline of my bra, me inching my hands up his shirt and feeling my way across the landscape of his chest—but not today.

Today I pull my shirt off, unhook my bra, and steal a kiss from Brian before he stands and pulls his own shirt off, kicks off his pants, and helps me with the rest of my clothes. Then he kneels by the couch, presses his hand between my breasts, spreads my knees, and lays the flat of his tongue against my clit.

Oh fuck—I have to grab a cushion and bite on it just to keep from shouting. He knows it, too. I can hear him laughing softly, feel him against my pussy, vibrations rocketing around me and sparking off each other as his tongue slips out again to trace my folds, dips lower and then sweeps up to circle my clit and suck, hard, right where I need him to.

Fuck, he knows this, he knows me, knows my body and my taste, and his fingertips tease my nipple while I start rising on the wave of him, barely remembering to keep quiet as I build higher and higher.

70

He doesn't let me come all the way—he knows I'm good for more than one if he times me right. He pulls away to put on a condom, and when I'm more reasonable I'll appreciate the thought, but right now I can't feel anything but the throbbing in my cunt that needs something else to happen, one more thing to get me up and over the hill and into my denied orgasm.

I'm writhing on the couch, trying to get anything to touch me, the cushions, the air, I don't care, and then finally, there's Brian, kneeling on the couch, lifting my leg over his thigh. His chest is dusted with the same salt and pepper as his hair, and his cock is hard against his stomach, darker than the rest of him, slick-looking under the condom. Just seeing him like this, staring down at me like somehow *I'm* the beautiful one, as though I'm the one with the body of the gods, makes all my blood rush down to where I desperately want us to connect.

I realize that I still have that cushion in my hands and wonder why. *Why am I touching anything other than him?* I throw it aside and drag him down to me. I want him, I need him inside me, that perfect cock filling my hole; his body rubbing mine and his head in my hands…I need it all. He opens his mouth and drinks my kisses like I'm water in the desert, my flavor still rich on his tongue. I taste like honey.

My hand joins his to guide him to my entrance, and then he pushes in, settling and resetting us on the couch until we're certain that the cushions won't squeak and that I won't shout too loudly.

With a foot braced on the floor and his arms around me, Brian fucks me slowly, with shallow thrusts that only draw him out an inch before he fills me completely again. My hands are in his hair, my legs around his waist, my heels digging into his ass—I can feel that all of him is concentrating on every part of me. The air between us gets hotter. I kiss him again, not caring if I reach his mouth or his jaw; I want to taste his sweat. He murmurs something I can't hear, and then I feel his hand between us, rubbing my clit just as he thrusts in again, and I'm cresting over, over, over that first mountain until I see stars.

"Beautiful Anna. You're gorgeous, so beautiful." I gradually come down from my high, drinking in the sound of Brian whispering as he slowly fucks me through it, still hard inside me—he hasn't come yet. He's pushing my hair back from my face, watching me with his heart in his eyes. It's a look that's becoming more familiar, even if we still haven't talked about it, but I think—I know—it's the same look I have.

I'm not ready to say anything just yet, though. I smile up at him, biting my lip, and then I squeeze him from the inside, gripping him with my inner self. He chokes, pauses in his rhythm, presses his forehead against my breast and groans, "Fuck," loudly enough that I have to shush him, giggling.

And then I squeeze him again.

Brian swears under his breath, something rough and fantastic, and lifts me bodily from the couch until I'm straddling him, my knees on either side of his lap, his cock somehow impossibly deeper inside me.

"Ride me," he says harshly against my breasts, "please," and the only answer I give him is to rise onto my knees and then slide back down his shaft again, gripping him as tightly as I can with my cunt when I reach the base. He gasps, just like that first time I touched him so many months ago, and buries his face against the side of my breast to cover his groan. I rise again as he begins to spread kisses over my breasts, and I drop just as his mouth closes around my nipple. He sucks, his tongue pressed against the peaked flesh, and my second orgasm takes me like an aftershock, all of the stimulation just too much to stop me: his mouth, his cock, the angle of his body against my clit, his hands in my hair, and even the way I can hear him breathing.

My orgasm triggers his. His hands leave my hair and grasp my hips, slamming my body to meet his ragged thrusts. It's perfect: raging, fiery, fast, everything hot and immediate and now, now, God, *fuck*—I kiss him hard, my arms tight around him and I bear down to try to take in as much of him as I can, to hold him inside me for as long as he'll have me.

He shuts his eyes and lets out a long, drawn out breath, holding me as tightly as I'm holding him. After a moment he relaxes, but he doesn't let go. He leans back against the couch, pulling me with him so I'm leaning against his chest with him still inside me. Gently, with a hand that's nearly shaking, he draws his fingers through the ends of my hair.

We're both breathing heavily. I can't see a clock from here, but it must nearly be time for him to leave. I wish it wasn't. I want him to stay. I want all of him, close and forever.

It's not really a new thought, but it's never been so concrete before. I think about how he looked at me earlier, with that heart-in-his-eyes look. I think about how often he's been doing that and how often I know I've been doing it too. How frequent our "play dates" have gotten, sure, but also how much time we spend together otherwise, just helping each other with our kids and being friends. Best friends.

I think about how much I really like Brian.

How much—God, how much I think I love him.

I push myself away from him, just a little bit, just enough so I can see his face. He's still running his hand through my hair. He's still inside me. I smile, and it feels like something I've never done before. "Hey," I start, and I touch his hair because I want to, and he's smiling back at me like I'm about to tell him the most amazing thing. Which I think I am. "I think," I say, "I think I…"

And down the hall, I hear the wail of my sixteen-month-old start up like a siren.

Talk about timing. *Ugh.* I thunk my head against Brian's shoulder, and he laughs and kisses my temple. I take a moment to snuggle him back, and then we're up, getting cleaned up, and Brian's helping me with the baby for a few short minutes before giving me a hot, fast kiss and leaving to get his kid from camp, and I think to myself, *There's no rush. Not about this.*

I'll tell him at our next play date.

Unleashed

Jen Lee

Water hissed up into the air every time Josie moved her finger. In the middle of a load of laundry, the hose connecting the washer to the water had begun to leak. She finally let the spray go, wrestled the washer far enough out from the wall to turn the water off, then slumped over the machine thinking, *Man, is this all my life is?* Work, home, bed, and up early the next day to do it all again, with an occasional crisis thrown in to remind her that she wasn't rich yet.

She stood up and stretched. Popping and creaking, she was also reminded that she was not as young as she used to be. Ruefully, she looked down at where her tits were before she had a child, and then lower, to where they were currently. *Damn!* It seemed like it had been ten years since someone had touched her boobs when they weren't being washed or used as a food source. While that may not be entirely accurate, it had been a very long time, and even longer since she'd been intimate with someone who actually satisfied her. *No use in crying over spilled breast milk,* she thought; wet laundry waited for no one.

Later that evening Josie stood in front of her bedroom mirror, naked. She looked at herself critically, assessing every lump, bump, and stretchmark. *Not bad, but sure could be better.* She sucked in her stomach and threw back her shoulders. Her breasts rested softly atop her rib cage, rippling with every breath. Her nipples puckered as she cupped the weight of her breasts, offering them to an imaginary lover. As she was boldly propositioning her invisible stud, her door burst open, and she shrieked and scrambled to cover up. Her son, the dog, and the cat tumbled through the doorway in a ball of paws and chaos. Her son looked up at her, now clutching her pajamas in front of herself, and curled his lip.

"What were you doing?" he asked. Ever since he first learned the basics of the birds and the bees three years earlier when he was nine, he seemed to analyze her every move like a suspicious prison warden—especially during "private" moments such as this.

"What I do is none of your business," she snapped, as she herded them out and slammed the door behind them. "And if my door is shut, you need to knock first!" Some days she felt like she had no privacy in her own house.

After her son finally went to sleep, Josie snuggled down in her bed. The house was quiet and she wanted to dream. Josie set it up in her mind: her fantasy lover would be a rugged man with a steady job, a big cock, and the desire to make her come however she wanted. A real fantasy! She drifted off to sleep with a sense of longing and desire thrumming through her exhausted mind.

*****

The next day Josie came home early from work to let the handyman in to fix the washer. A knock on the door interrupted her as she threw her hair up into her customary at-home ponytail. She looked through her screen door and a curious heated flush started to creep through her body. The handyman loomed on her porch, gripping a battered toolbox in one meaty hand. He was tall; she tilted her head back as she gave him a long look from the tips of his battered work boots to the top of his hat. Her eyes strayed back to his huge hands: scarred and work worn, they fascinated her. He said something and she stared at his mouth dumbly.

"Excuse me, are you Mrs. Allen?" he repeated, his deep voice low and rumbling. He probably assumed that she had already been drinking and had forgotten her own name.

She quickly opened the door to allow him in. "It's Ms. Allen. Josie. I'm not married, I'm hungry." *Crap!* She winced at her *faux pas* as a small half smile curved his lips upward.

"Well, Josie, I'm Joe Sheppard. You called about your washer, and maybe you should eat...if you're hungry, that is." One eyebrow arched over the twinkle lighting his eyes.

"Come on in." She mentally slapped the loser sign to her forehead as she led him to the washer.

"Obviously, this is the washer; the hose thingy sprung a leak yesterday." She waved her hand in the direction of the broken hose and lost her train of thought. He had bent over the washer and the material of his canvas cargo pants cupped his fine ass lovingly, causing Josie's mouth to dry up. She had the sudden urge to be bold and sweep her hand up between his legs to fondle his cock.

"The hose needs to be replaced, there's a pin-hole leak in it," he said. Josie's eyes widened as she remembered that they were supposed to be talking about the washer hose.

"Okay, go ahead, do what you have to do." Josie's voice had dropped an octave and she licked her lips nervously.

Having noticed her unusual behavior, he stood and stared at her, puzzlement on his face.

What am I thinking? she mused. Her libido was running away with her common sense. Josie shook her head to clear her thoughts and turned away. She had to put some space between them.

"I am going to run to get this part and I'll be back in about twenty minutes," he said, heading for the door.

From across the room, Josie turned to him and replied, "Okay, sex you later then." *Shit, shit, shit!* Josie covered her face with her hands, embarrassment swamping her. She heard him chuckle as he turned to leave. After peeking out from between her fingers to make sure he was gone, Josie stomped her foot, frustrated that she wasn't being as calm and sophisticated in her real life as she had been in her fantasy last night. She decided that a cold shower was just the thing.

Ten minutes later, refreshed and refocused, she was brushing out her hair when she heard the front door open.

"Moooommmmm, where are you?" her son bellowed at the top of his lungs.

Sighing, she threw on a tank top and shorts before he burst in on her naked again.

76

"Don't yell, I'm right here." Josie walked into the hallway and crossed her arms over her braless breasts.

"I'm heading over to Mike's house to play video games. I'll be back by nine thirty?" he said, with a question in his voice.

"Nine o'clock, it's a school night," Josie countered.

"No homework, nine thirty, and I'll even take the dog," he wheedled sweetly.

"Fine, no later or you'll be grounded." Her voice trailed after him as he and the dog ran out the door. Josie relished that it would be a quiet night and reminded herself that she'd better put on underwear before the handyman returned. As she turned toward her bedroom, she saw his truck pull back in and groaned. Her wet hair had started to dry in curls and waves around her head, and she had no time to put it up. He knocked and she ran to the door with a polite smile on her face to let him in. He was still just as good looking. Josie repeated the mantra in her head: *calm, cool, and collected...focus!*

As he passed by her to step inside, he took a deep breath and inhaled. He could smell her, clean and sweet, warm and delicious. Her long, dark hair swayed as much as her hips as he watched her, following her toward the washer.

"Were you able to get the part that was needed?" she asked, turning to face him. Her tight, white tank top outlined her taut nipples and he swallowed hard. *No bra! I wonder if she's wearing panties?*

"The part, the part...yeah I was able to get it, no problem, and it shouldn't take me long to change it out." He was babbling and he knew it. A grown, mature man shouldn't be so nervous when faced with an attractive, braless, hungry woman. He bent over the washer and proceeded to fiddle with the hose, distracted by listening to her movements behind him in the kitchen.

Sweat beaded on his forehead as he reached for a wrench and looked her way. Josie was bent over looking for something in a cabinet, her round ass in the air, the thin material of her shorts glued to its contours. *No underwear,* he thought. Josie was not a tall woman; she was short and curvy. Generously curvy. He liked that in a woman, liked that it gave you something to hold on to. Yes, he liked what he saw, all soft curves, and real tits that jiggled under her tank top as she reached for a glass from a cupboard. Josie had short, muscular legs that would grip a man tightly between them. The rounded mound of her stomach would make a soft landing a man could get comfortable on. Joe groaned silently as these thoughts chased through his head and blood pooled in his cock.

"Are you okay?" Josie asked him. "You look a little flushed, can I get you some water?"

"Water? Oh, yeah, water would be good, thanks." He stood up from where he'd been crouched by the back of the washer and stepped closer to her. Up close he could see her big, brown eyes with the little crinkles at the corners. Her lips were plump, as were her cheeks. She gave him a little smile and handed him a glass.

Grab the bull by the horns and ride! Do it Josie, where are your balls? Josie was having a quick-fire mental conversation with herself as she stared at his hand gripping that glass. A bead of condensation plopped down off the glass and disappeared under the neckline of his t-shirt, making her think even more about his strong chest. Finished, he extended the glass toward her.

Josie reached for the glass and her courage. *Be bold Josie,* she told herself. "Are you single?" she blurted. That had come out rather baldly. Josie forced herself to continue looking straight at him and waited for his answer.

"Yes," was his simple answer. He knew now, without question, what she wanted; her nipples had snagged his attention once again, and he couldn't drag his eyes away.

She stepped around the end of the counter and got closer to him; she only came up to the middle of his broad chest. Josie kept her eyes on his as she slid her hand up his chest to palm the back of his neck. She stood on her toes and inhaled, moaning low in her throat; he smelled like something she wanted to lick. He pulled her closer to his chest, his huge arms caging her close. Her hard nipples bored into him as he leaned down to kiss her. Those big hands of his slid down her back, cupping her generous ass and bringing her even closer to him. He settled his lips over hers and plunged his tongue into her mouth, stroking her tongue with his, mimicking what his cock would do.

Deprived of a man's touch for so long, Josie eagerly flung herself off the cliff. He was nibbling on her earlobe and the sensitive side of her neck as she threw her head back, wantonly offering herself up to his mouth. His fingers had crept under the leg of her shorts and were stroking the crease between her thigh and her pussy. Josie rubbed herself against his leg, rocking her hips as she rode his thigh, trying to alleviate the throb in her clit.

She broke away to pull him toward her bedroom. No words were spoken; none were needed. Josie was determined to follow through, and for once, to enjoy something just for her. Josie yanked back the covers on her bed and faced him.

"Take off your clothes," he commanded. A little shiver went through her as he took charge. Josie moved to strip off her tank top and shove her shorts down her legs. Self-consciously, she crossed her hands over her pubic mound and sucked in her stomach. He had taken off his own clothes pretty quickly and she took in the sight of him. His chest was lightly furred, his legs long and sturdy. Josie inspected his package and liked what she saw. His shaft was wide and thick, the head of his cock was broad, and his balls were huge and tight. Josie squeezed her legs together as she became wet and achy.

"Stop trying to cover up and come here," he said, taking her hand and drawing her closer. Her large tits spilled into his big hands as he pinched and tweaked her nipples, making them jut out. He bent his head and sucked one hard nipple into the warm, wet cavern of his mouth. Josie arched her back, pressing her nipple closer to his teeth and tongue. He moved his head to treat the nipple of her other breast to the same. Josie was on fire, his mouth felt so good and she loved the feel of his teeth scraping across her nipple.

"Bite it harder," she told him. He readily complied with her order, taking her nipple between his teeth and biting down, not too hard, but with just enough pressure so that she felt the sensation streak through her.

"You like that, do you?" he asked, as she bucked her hips against his hard cock.

"More," she whimpered. Instead of giving her more he moved toward the bed, pulling her beside him as he lay on his back, his cock jutting up from his body, boldly bobbing toward her. Taking the bull by the horn, Josie curled her hand around it, pumping her fist up and down.

"Suck it," he ordered. Josie leaned forward and flicked out her tongue on the bulbous head, taking a little taste. She swirled her tongue around and around and licked the length of his shaft, dipping lower to swipe her tongue over his ball sac. Moving back up the length of him, she sucked him into her mouth, pumping her fist in a counter rhythm. She swallowed the length of him down her throat, enjoying his hands in her hair that encouraged her to continue. She bobbed up and down intently, focused on his hard cock in her mouth.

"Unless you want me to come in your mouth, you need to stop." He groaned as if in pain when she finally released him from the suction of her mouth. Josie swiped a hand across her lips, hungry for more.

"What do you like? What will make you come?" he asked her. Josie paused to consider this before she answered him. Nobody had ever asked her that before. Her last lover was selfish, hogging all the orgasms for himself. He never bothered to find out what might make her come. What did she really want?

"I want to ride you," Josie answered, surprising herself with her own boldness.

"Get on." He slid over to the middle of the bed to give her room. She scrambled up his body, climbing him like a tree. Before she got caught up in fucking his brains out she reached over him to grab a condom from her secret stash. She tore open the package with her teeth and rolled it over him.

The first thrust was a slow slide that felt so good, she moaned aloud. It had been quite a while for her so it was a very tight fit, but she worked her pussy against his thick cock until she had it all in. Forcing away her feelings of self-consciousness, Josie rose straight up and moved her hips in a circle over his cock as he watched her. She looked down at his chest and placed her hands flat for balance. She was ready to ride! Josie was moving her hips and getting slicker and slicker as she rode him. She could feel him thickening even more inside her and he leaned up to suck a hard nipple into his mouth.

Abruptly, he said, "Wait, stop for minute." She looked down at him and froze, confused.

80

"Let's switch it up, I don't want to come too soon." He flipped her onto her back before she could protest...not that she was going to. He settled his hips in between her soft thighs and fed his hard cock into her wetness. He pulled her feet up to rest on his shoulders so he could plunge in deep. Josie undulated her hips in time to his hard thrusts, his ball sac making a rhythmic slapping noise against her ass cheeks.

As he was thrusting, he began to circle his thumb against her clit, wringing a lusty moan from deep in her throat. *Oh yeah*, Joe relished, as he continued to slide his cock in and out of the warm, tight clutch of her pussy, *this is the way to spend the afternoon!* A tightening began in his balls as his orgasm approached. She hadn't come yet and he wasn't ready for the fun to end, so he slowed his thrusts, holding her legs up by her ankles. Josie moved her hips, seeking his hard cock as he slowly pulled it out of her. She looked up at him and waited. Thankfully, she didn't have to wait for long.

"On your hands and knees, put that sweet ass in the air for me."

Josie rolled over and arched her back deeply, ass in the air. She felt a sharp sting, and then warmth spreading across her cheeks as he gave her a little slap on the ass.

"Do you need a spanking? Have you been naughty?" Joe rasped as he swatted her again, kneading the flesh of her ass in between slaps. *Smack!* Another slap and Josie was gasping out loud and pushing her ass closer to his hand.

"Tell me what you want," he said. Another teasing slap caused a jolt of warmth to shoot through her whole body.

Joe had pushed a broad fingertip between her legs and was rhythmically stroking her clit. He enjoyed seeing her ass pink and begging to be spanked...if she would only beg a little, it would be the cherry on top.

Josie was getting closer to a monster orgasm as Joe continued to stroke her clit and smack her ass. She was so close!

"If you're not going to tell me what you want, I guess I'll have to stop and go back to fixing your washer," Joe teased, as he withdrew his finger and began to back up off the bed.

Josie hated to beg for anything; she prided herself on her independence. She buried her head in the pillow, frustrated that she wanted this man and that her body wanted—no, *needed*—this physical release. Another sharp slap to her ass brought her head up and around to look at him over her shoulder. He was staring at her ass intently as his rough hands smoothed the sting of his previous slap from her skin. He leaned over and as she waited for him to kiss her plump ass cheek, she felt a sharp, sudden sting and realized he had bitten her! She yelped in surprise.

"Nice and juicy, just the way I like it." He smiled a little and she felt a liquid heat pool between her thighs. Head down, Josie pushed her ass back toward his hard cock, until the head of his erection was nudging her opening.

"Nope, none for you, until you ask nicely," Joe said as he moved his hips back a fraction of an inch. His fingers had returned to her clit and were slowly building her back up toward a screaming orgasm.

Josie was stubborn, but it had been so long since she felt like this, she was literally going to burst apart at the seams. She rocked her hips, grinding herself against his fingers, trying to get some relief.

"Naughty girl, you know what you have to do," Joe crooned as he spanked her ass again and again. She was so close, but she needed something more.

"Fuck me," Josie ground out between clenched teeth.

"No, that's too general; you need to be more specific." Joe was close to giving in, but he was determined to hear her say it.

"Fuck me with your cock," she pleaded.

"Tell me how you want it, Josie." He brought his cock closer to the hot, liquid warmth of her pussy, brushing against her lightly.

"Hard and deep, fuck me hard and deep, now!" Josie spit out her demand as he plowed forward and sank into her.

"Since you asked, I will give you what want." Joe grinned and tightened his grip on her hips. He shifted one leg, putting his foot flat on the bed to give himself more leverage. He slid into her further, plunging deeper. Josie moaned and moved herself back and forth on his erection. Joe could feel his orgasm tightening his ball sac, growing closer, and he began to move faster.

Josie felt him going deeper, hitting a sensitive spot inside her; she felt him reach under her to stroke her clit in time with his hips. Between his cock stroking her inside and his finger on her clit, she tensed up. He could feel her pussy begin to clamp down as her orgasm swelled and vibrated through her. The tighter she got around him, the more his cock swelled, and he started to come too.

"Fuck yeah, I'm coming, ohhhh shit," Joe groaned, as his fingers sank into the flesh of her hips and he shuddered through his orgasm.

Josie could feel his cock throb as her own orgasm gripped her and made her moan long and loud. She continued to rock against his cock as they both strained against each other to wring out the last bits of feeling from their mutual orgasm.

Joe rested a minute, willing his heart to slow down. His cock softened and he pulled out from her reluctantly. Josie took a deep breath and collapsed on the bed. Sweaty and satisfied, she didn't want to move. She felt the bed dip as he lay next to her, breathing heavily.

Josie opened one eye to look at him beside her and wondered if it was possible for her washer to break at least once a week. She snuck a look at her alarm clock on the bedside stand. Only 7:00. Two-and-a-half more hours of uninterrupted Josie time. She briefly wondered if she had the balls, then quickly decided that she did.

Josie slid her hand down his stomach and stroked his twitching cock; he was already getting hard again.

"I think you have been a very good boy, however, you still need to be punished," she said with a grin. She leaned over to give him a long, hot kiss. "This time it won't be me that's begging," Josie promised, and gave him an evil little smile.

It was a lucky thing that she had broken her washer; maybe tomorrow her dryer would need to be serviced. Wait, it was her that needed to be serviced. Good thing he was a handy man!

A Moment With You

Alice Bright

It was a Wednesday night, and Marissa made chicken for dinner. It felt like the millionth time. She had made this meal so many times, in fact, that she could practically do it in her sleep. Without blinking or hesitation, she chopped up the chicken breast and dropped it into the frying pan with a dollop of butter. It didn't take long for the meat to start sizzling. As she added the appropriate spices, she tried to tune out the sounds of yelling and screaming coming from upstairs. The boys were fighting again. The boys were always fighting.

"Dinner!" She yelled, as she carefully put a plate of chicken, vegetables, and rice at each person's spot on the table. A stampede, or something like it, started to happen on the stairs as her two four-year-olds tumbled down the steps on top of one another.

"Thanks, Mommy!" They yelled in unison as they sat at the table and began to inhale their dinner. Within minutes, they were through. Pushing their seats back, they left their empty plates on the table and ran upstairs to finish playing before bedtime. Marissa observed the small pile of rice on the floor that surrounded each chair. With a sigh, she grabbed a washcloth and started to clean up the dinner mess. James would be home soon and she wanted the house to look nice for him.

*****

Marissa woke when her husband slammed the front door. Her nightstand alarm clock displayed 10:04 pm. It had been another late night. Being married to a soldier, she had gotten used to going to bed alone. Being a mother, she had gotten used to going to bed at 8:00 pm. It hadn't been on purpose, she noted, prying herself out from beneath the children, who had fallen asleep in her bed, but at the end of the day, she just couldn't find the energy to do anything relaxing for herself, much less try to wait up for James.

She slipped downstairs quietly, painfully aware of her messy hair and rumpled clothes. She wished that, just once, she had somehow kept enough energy to wait up for her husband. Tonight had been just the same as all the others: falling asleep while reading bedtime stories, still wearing her clothes that were stained from dinner and finger paint.

"Hey sweetie," James greeted her with a kiss. He was still in his uniform. He made it look great even after all these years. "Thanks for saving me some dinner."

Marissa wrapped her arms around her husband's narrow waist. She was jealous on some level that he got to exercise as part of his job. He always seemed to stay in shape effortlessly. She glanced down at her own flabby belly. Laden with scars from carrying twins, she felt forever self-conscious of it. Forever maimed. As if he could tell she needed to be reassured, James returned her gentle embrace.

His fingers slid ever so slightly beneath the back of her shirt and pulled her closer to him, imparting his desire for her to return his touches.

"You look really sexy," he said with a grin, kissing her again. Her hard nipples protruded under her thin t-shirt, begging him to take a peek. Even after all these years, she still managed to turn him on just as quickly as when they first started dating.

"I missed you tonight," she said, leaning up toward him. "I always miss you."

"I missed you, too, baby," he purred into her ear, sending a quiver throughout her body. "And I need you, now."

"I need you, too," she responded, suddenly more ready than ever to forget about the mundane sameness of her day. If anyone could make her feel like the young, wild woman she once was, it was James.

Without any more urging, he slid his hands under the front of her shirt and squeezed her supple breasts. Marissa let out a soft moan as James pulled her shirt off completely and tossed it to the floor. Her nipples were even harder than before as he leaned down and began to softly suckle at each one, licking and tantalizing the entire breast until Marissa grabbed his head and pulled it up to hers.

Shoving her tongue against his, she kissed him deeply and passionately. James was the most fantastic man she'd ever met, and she had met quite a few men in her life. He somehow managed to know just what she needed, when she needed it, and how she needed it. Tonight was no exception.

James reached down and pulled off her sweatpants and panties. They landed in a pile on the floor next to her shirt. James lifted his naked wife to the counter so that she was facing him.

"You're naked," he commented. "Now, what am I going to do about that?"

She smiled and grabbed his belt, pulling him closer. Gently, carefully, she unbuttoned his jacket and let it fall to the floor. Kissing him, she pulled his shirt off and his pants quickly followed. His dick was already hard when his boxers hit the floor. He kicked them away and grabbed his cock, rubbing it quickly.

"I love to watch you," Marissa kissed his neck softly, making her way down his arm until she reached his elbow, but before she could get any further he grabbed her hair and pulled her head back. Without a word, she wrapped her legs around his body and pulled him into her. His cock slid quickly into her waiting pussy. She was ready for him, as he was for her. She moaned, softly, as he began to thrust. She leaned back onto her elbows on the counter, allowing herself to be taken. It was moments like these that she truly felt alive, truly felt amazing, truly felt like the most beautiful woman in the world.

James continued to touch her, all of her, as he reminded her vigorously why he married her, why he couldn't get enough of her, why he found her irresistible. His hands made their way up and down her body again and again until finally, he couldn't hold back anymore and exploded deep inside of her. Marissa melted beneath the push of his climax, embracing him as he

86

came. She kissed him softly on the cheek, running her fingers through his hair.

When he had finished, he lifted her up and carried her to the living room couch. Pushing the toys and laundry to the floor, he leaned her back on the sofa and knelt before her.

"Mmm, look at that pussy," he whispered, leaning in close. "So sweet, all for me." Marissa didn't have to tell him what to do. James delved forward into her waiting lips and began licking, sucking, and nibbling at her. She wriggled with pleasure beneath his tongue. He knew this was her favorite way to come. It didn't take long for her to start biting her lips, to start holding her breath, to grab his head and push it deeper into her sex until she, too, climaxed. With a soft moan, she collapsed backward onto the sofa, exhausted and relaxed.

"I think you're amazing," he whispered, climbing up next to her and kissing her softly.

"I love you," she told him, still surprised that even after all this time, he could make her forget about her long day. He always knew just how to make her feel wanted, desired, romanced. He always knew just how to make her excited, just how to get her riled up.

James grabbed a pair of pajama pants from the laundry pile and rustled up some clean pajamas for Marissa as well. Once dressed, he grabbed her hand and led her slowly up the stairs to their bedroom. Their bed was still full of their children, but they managed to find space for themselves even amongst the chaos. As Marissa leaned her head onto his shoulder, she closed her eyes and smiled. It had been a perfect day.

About the Authors

The stories in "Ignite" were written by ten talented authors. Some have been published numerous times, enjoying strong, established careers as writers, and others are newly discovered talent, for whom this is their first published work.

Michael Bracken
Alice Bright
Shenoa Carroll-Bradd
Katherine Crighton
Julianna Darling
Kelly Lawrence
Jen Lee
J.R. Read
Lizzie Richards
Lori Verni-Fogarsi

We encourage you to visit our website, where you can learn a bit about each author, what inspired their story, and how to connect with them!

www.BrickstonePublishing.com/IgniteAuthors

About Brickstone Publishing

Brickstone Publishing is a small press committed to building a solid foundation for books and their authors. We are not a huge publishing house...nor do we try to be. Rather, we publish an average of one or two books each year, with a focus on quality. Quality authors, professional editing, and top-notch cover art are backed by our small staff who are well-versed in both the traditional and more contemporary aspects of the industry. All of our books are available in both paper and e-book formats.

Lori Verni-Fogarsi, who compiled the stories in *Ignite*, has been an author, speaker, and small business consultant since 1995. She has been featured in major media including *Lifetime Women's Network*, the *My Carolina Today Show*, and *Boston Globe Forums Live.* Her public speaking has occurred at many prestigious venues including *North Carolina State University, Nassau Community College,* and many more.

She has received three awards for her novels, *Momnesia* and *Unexpecting*, and her nonfiction, *Everything You Need to Know About House Training Puppies and Adult Dogs,* continues to be one of the most highly recommended in its genre since 2005.

Lori is a happily married mom of two, stepmom of two more, and has two cats, both rotten. She is very excited to bring you the carefully selected stories in *Ignite*, and enjoys getting to know her readers via social media and in person. She invites you to get to know her, and learn about past and future projects at **www.LoriTheAuthor.com**.

We invite you to learn more about our books, our staff, and connect with all of our authors at www.BrickstonePublishing.com.

If you enjoyed "Ignite,"

you'll love what's coming out next!

You can stay updated on our new releases
by following us on Facebook, Twitter, or joining
our mailing list at our website!

www.Facebook.com/BrickstonePublishing

Twitter: @BrickstonePub

Website: www.BrickstonePublishing.com

✓ **Contemporary women's fiction**
✓ **Nonfiction**
✓ **Tasteful erotic fiction**

28122165R00051

Made in the USA
Lexington, KY
06 December 2013